Gogol's Disco

Paavo Matsin

GOGOL'S DISCO

Translated from the Estonian by Adam Cullen

DALKEY ARCHIVE PRESS
McLean, IL / Dublin

Originally published by Viljandi, Lepp ja Nagel as *Gogoli disko* in 2015.

Copyright © by Paavo Matsin in 2015.

Translation copyright © by Adam Cullen, 2019.

First Dalkey Archive edition, 2019.

ISBN: 978-1-943150-38-0

Dalkey Archive Press
McLean, IL / Dublin

Co-funded by the
Creative Europe Programme
of the European Union

Supported by the Estonian Minister of Culture and the Cultural Endowment of Estonia.

Printed on permanent/durable acid-free paper.
www.dalkeyarchive.com

Contents

All flew and rushed about looking for the
philosopher.

Nikolai Gogol, "Viy"

Hither, come hither!
The porridge is here;
The table I've spread,
Come taste of my cheer.

Wilhelm Hauff, "Little Muck"

Gogol's Disco

Part I

Konstantin Opiatovich

The pickpocket Konstantin Opiatovich kept certain daily routines he had acquired over many years spent in penitentiaries. Having ironed his pants in the morning with a heated tin mug; polished his shoes using a small, worn scrap of velvet he always kept on his person; and filled his pockets with plenty of the bread crusts he dried on the windowsill, he would then take an early tram to the last stop. Stepping off the paved street onto a narrow path of cobblestones (carefully, to avoid puddles), he jauntily made his way towards the old Jewish cemetery. Jews were known for their stubbornness and honoring of traditions. They adhered to many ancient rules and, therefore, their shadowy cemetery was an ideal place for a respectable pickpocket to begin his day. His former yard-mate, who was an Odessan Jew, had informed him of quite a lot of interesting tidbits concerning the tiny, persecuted nation's secret customs. Opiatovich couldn't remember it all any more, but the pebbles placed on the gravestones instead of flowers, and that entire fairytale world with a miniature gate meant only for the rabbi, had a somehow invigorating effect before he attended to his daily job. Later, after working the tram, it would be too dangerous to ride back to the last stop purely to take a stroll. Whenever he tired of the noisy passengers and pinching from purses, Opiatovich would often relax by walking between tram stops and feeding pigeons with the bread crusts. Yet here in the deserted world of silent Hebrew-language tablets, he would, if possible, carry out a calm introduction to the business about to begin. Stopping next to a gravestone he picked by intuition, he would place upon its dewy surface a tiny stone scooped up casually from the path. In doing so, Opiatovich practiced a specific and vital skill for a *karmanchik*: digital mobility. He would also listen to the silence and to himself. At the same time, he never violated the age-old rule of thieving when scooping up the stones: he was all too familiar with the fact that even the most sentimental pickpocket should never lift anything heavier than a wallet.

In the wake of recent events, in which Tsarist Russia had once again annexed the Baltic states of Estonia, Latvia, and Lithuania, even the provincial town of Viljandi was awash with changes—good and bad alike, of course. Take for example the trophy tram that had been transported from Krakow or Warsaw or elsewhere—rails, depot, engines and all—after the terrible battles with Poland. The town's pensioners applauded the novelty and soon, every resident was in the habit of taking free rides on the unprecedented means of transport that the beaks of a double-headed eagle had deposited there. Finely calibrated by Muscovite specialists, it now ran very naturally from one end of Viljandi to the other, coping with every topographical anomaly, entering a transparent modern tunnel under the lake and speeding across the castle ruins with the bravado of an American railroad in order to carry the ever-swelling population to the new residential areas under construction on the outskirts. Opiatovich generally steered clear of politics (a proper thief never collaborates with any regime), but the tram was extremely beneficial in several ways. Thus, to employ technical terms, Opiatovich could proudly state that when the tsarist eagle came back to roost in the region, he, as a former sident and—to the best of his abilities—current *stilyaga*, suffered no great *depresyak*, but simply did what he did best. The giant swing of history simply was repeatedly to circle the same beam over his lifetime, so it would seem. Furthermore, he'd managed to make nice friends at a used bookstore downtown, where it was nice to kick back and converse like human beings after the day's scuffles on the tram.

Musing, Opiatovich strolled a short circuit to appreciate the scattered gravestones that resembled an abandoned game of dominos—sunken and leaning here forward, there back, reminding him of the good old days when he belonged to a chic Riga gang that spent its evenings playing those endless black-and-white games. Similarly, real dominos were often associated with the deceased! Once, for example, he'd wound up at a gaming table in a bunker in Riga's Pārdaugava district, where he'd discovered a sheath nailed beneath the table so one could furtively pull a knife if things went south. In his younger days, Opiatovich had indeed worn a white scarf and carried a Finnish blade, a *finka*, but had never openly drawn a sharp weapon against another person. With the exception of the sharpened coins he used to slit purses, of course. Now, all that remained were the trams and the old women returning from the market with their scant coins . . . but luckily, also the tunes! How wonderful it was to whistle as he walked in this kingdom of shadows, be it the classic "Murka," "The Prosecutor's Daughter," or the particularly funereal "Sweet Berry." Life wasn't actually all that bad! He wouldn't have minded a wife, but he who is unlucky in love . . . Only yesterday, he'd been tracked down by the young female thief known by the telling nickname Murka, who had asked his permission to do a little purloining around town. She was pretty like an evil princess, and the local boys were said to be afraid of her already—rumor had it she'd pluck the bread from your hand and was as talented as the devil . . . Oh, he could use a woman like that as his wife, indeed he could! Naturally, he'd granted his permission—it had never been in any doubt.

Thereafter, Opiatovich's thoughts drifted to the queen of games: billiards, a contest of immense philosophy, greater even than any bespectacled old professor could ever concoct! Take, for instance, the *durak*—a ball that rolls randomly into a pocket, the same way anyone at all might end up in the wrong place, suffer a crippling blow, and . . . meet their demise! Or, viewed from the opposite angle, a man may enjoy great and unparalleled fortune even though he himself seems to play no significant part in it, simply standing agape, staring at the world like a lamb fetched to the slaughter. But then, suddenly, a shot rings out . . . and you're buried either in gold or in the ground! Opiatovich's former cellmate had told him that the Jews bury their dead quickly and always in a seated position. Again, what an interesting fact! How rich life is! It turns out that underground all the Jews are seated as if on a tram, riding off in some direction, toward Judgement Day, Jerusalem, or whatever end awaits them there. Of course, there couldn't be any thieves on those underground trams . . . But wait, wait—what did that make grave robbers, then? Not long ago, there'd been an article in the bilingual provincial newspaper telling of how restorers from St. Petersburg's Hermitage had been working on the church in Suure-Jaani, just to the north of Viljandi, and had drunk all the embalming fluid from a glass container holding the old Baltic German's heart, which they had found in the grave obelisk! Yes, life was certainly interesting, no doubt about it! So very unexpected! So very rich!

Mulling these thoughts and chuckling to himself at the start of that beautiful day in the tiny imperial town of Viljandi, pickpocket Konstantin Opiatovich headed back to the tram stop. He paused for a moment next to the large sepulcher depicting a menorah, the seven-branched Jewish candelabrum, where he always polished his shoes with the scrap of velvet. Today, he even had to remove one shoe to dislodge a tiny stone from the tread. As he lifted his eyes, Opiatovich was struck dumb by the unusual color of a certain bush. It was as red as a blazing fire against the surrounding greenery!

The Stranger

The tram screeched to an awful halt, clattering like a tambourine left hanging around a bandit's neck after a night of heavy revelry. To his great surprise, the pickpocket noticed the tram wasn't empty: seated across from the middle door was an individual fully wrapped in a frayed, faded brown scarf. On his head, the odd *stilyaga* wore a brimmed cap with astrakhan trimming, which resembled an old-fashioned accordion or a gigantic cloth snail shell. Around the seat, and in spite of the fact that the tram was still running its first circuits of the day, the floor was already so dreadfully sandy that Opiatovich was forced to execute a nimble rhumba-like sidestep as he passed the eccentric. Nutcases such as him were not his forte, as their unpredictability could only cause problems. However, since it was obvious that the ghost of a man had boarded at the previous stop, i.e. the new Russian Orthodox cemetery, Opiatovich—a professional—decided to take the risk. There is no one in the world more careless and preoccupied than a person wrapped up in corpses and funerals! Everyone on this side of mortality inevitably dupes the grieving and the bleary-eyed, from the coffin salesman and the gravedigger to the old tuba player who, reeling from the heavy scent of incense, insists on receiving his payment. And those imbeciles pay up, of course! They weep and they pay up! Not to mention the cynical caterers and the whole gamut of professional wake organizers. The business is truly burgeoning. Such impious jackals left barely anything for the honest thief! Still, one had to try!

Opiatovich sat behind the man and was immediately struck by a sweet, musty smell—an unusual mixture of incense and an elderly man's intimate ailments. Fighting nausea, more out of curiosity than greed, he slipped a hand into a pocket of the stranger's plaid coat. Oh-ho . . . it was lined with luxurious fur . . . but filled with sand! Startled, he withdrew his hand as he realized the stranger was mumbling to himself. The thief was able to make out two phrases: something had happened too soon, and someone had been warned. Over and over, the deranged man murmured the word . . . malaria! Then, the lunatic began shuddering with increasing intensity and, by an unbelievable stroke of luck, his bulging leather wallet dropped to the floor next to his seat, as thick as a cachalot. Opiatovich spontaneously started whistling the tune of "Murka."

Bully J. Badenov

Two older men had settled onto folding chairs on the sidewalk in front of the used bookstore on Castle Street, Viljandi's sole thoroughfare, where the narrowness of the medieval old town had been preserved and natural daylight was uncommon. Sipping from cups of hot tea, both rested their elbows on the thick, worn iron handrail behind them, which had been installed probably even before the previous imperial era to protect the display window. Adjacent to the little shop, which resembled a garden of delights, was a mildew-glazed alleyway leading into an overgrown courtyard where an unusual To Rent sign (still only in Estonian, for some reason) hung above the padlocked door to a cellar bar. Also taking into account the balcony above the men's heads, which boasted a couple of grand balustrades but was otherwise in a state of dreadful disrepair, and the shattered glass panes in the door of the shuttered puppet theater directly across from them, it was clear that the former main street's golden days lay somewhere in the distant past. The entire street felt like a gloomy, gray-haired *mamochka-mamashake*, who, leaning against a window frame as if resting on eternity, is forever awaiting the homecoming of her long-since convicted and executed son.

The thinner of the two, who weighed a mere 85 pounds, wore a stain-splattered tie, and was nicknamed Arkasha, was squeezing a plastic bag between his knees. He never let it out of his sight, as it contained all his earthly possessions (which mainly consisted of cheap underclothes). Arkasha's whole life had been luckless: he lived in perpetual separation from family and a proper lunch, or, as his friends would say, "Our Arkasha survives on music." For the last few years, he had been keeping his head above water thanks to underground recordings in which he delivered heartfelt renditions of classic songs about an officer's honor, the Russia he had lost, the woeful path of the émigré, and similar topics. Even the famous "Murka," a rendition of which we just had an opportunity to hear in the form of Konstantin Opiatovich's mild and cheerful whistling when he noticed an enticing *bumashnik* land on the floor of the tram, was included in Arkasha's golden repertoire and was, in fact, his specialty, his *koronaya*. The ditty told of a new gang arriving in Odessa, led by the revolver-wielding female thief named Murka. Tending to the technical end of the old-fashioned music business was Arkasha's present tablemate and good friend Bully J. Badenov. After the local Ugala Theater closed down,

Badenov cleverly arranged for the institution's entire array of sound equipment to be stored in one room of the communal apartment on the upstairs floor of the building that housed the bookstore. Consequently, he usually slept right there in front of the main door next to Arkasha; not upstairs in his rented space. Bully J.'s room was a spectacle all of its own. Russian and American flags hung prominently alongside autographed posters with personal dedications by Vysotsky and Presley. The latter had once even sent Badenov an official invitation to visit! The Soviet bureaucrats had initially laughed in his face when he submitted the document, but to the surprise of all, he was permitted to leave. The rest of Badenov's lair was occupied by record players, all kinds of sound equipment, vinyl records, and odd musical souvenirs he'd acquired abroad. Wonderous tales were told about Bully J.'s short-lived emigration to America, though all he himself would comment was that everything had been truly designer-chic. One's initial impression that total chaos reigned among the tangled extension cords and plug sockets was nevertheless false, as each and every object rested neatly in its rightful place. Bully J. believed that vinyl records had zero tolerance for familiarity, so to deter any risk of destruction, he stored his rarest specimens with the record and cover kept in separate boxes. His most prized possessions, however, were the underground records cut in that very same dark den on X-ray films still showing bones and all, which he'd also peddled quite successfully abroad. Bully J. felt pity for the recently deceased

Republic of Estonia, because in truth, he despised the totalitarian regimes that had prevented him from dedicating himself fully to his true calling and hobby: studying early rock and roll, a.k.a. "ancient" rock and roll; or, if you wish, pre-rock-and-roll rock and roll. On the whole, however, he was at peace. He knew that although undeserved oblivion had befallen many a great talent, fate had sent Arkady Dmitriyevich a.k.a. Arkasha, a national and ancient-rock-and-roll great, to cross his path before he, a hopeless romantic and authentic old-school producer-poet-collector, ultimately met his demise. Conversations with the vibrant soul that was Arkasha always demonstrated how true giftedness will gradually accumulate social status and designer-chic. Every moment spent with him made Bully J. sigh in joy and blush to remember the time before they met. Back then, he had spent his miserable days sitting in his musical garage, conjuring up strange, ineffective, additional verses or false refrains for his favorite songs. He hadn't dared to dream of ever enjoying a pretty wife or an intellectual companion. Nevertheless, an incredible guitar-pluck of fate had introduced him to Arkasha, to that divinely-ordained chic *muzykant*-Beatle-*stilyaga*!

Arkady Dmitriyevich Severny

Badenov could recall their first meeting down to the finest detail. He had just sat down with Vasya Kolyugin—Viljandi's leading Beatles aficionado—to discuss various future options for erecting a Beatles temple by the lake. The bearded Vasya had arrived like a saint and founder of a church, carrying a bizarre model made out of clay and a soccer ball that had been sliced in half. One side was meant to symbolize the world, the other love! They were in the communal apartment's communal kitchen when there came a knock on the door and a drab individual, wearing a gray suit and carrying a plastic bag, asked to see Bully J. The host showed the stranger to his studio/communal/multipurpose room and asked him to wait; however, he completely forgot his guest while discussing and debating temple affairs with Vasya. Suddenly (they'd just progressed to the topic of colors for the planned sanctuary and were arguing over whether the dome symbolizing love should be purple or pink), they heard someone had set the needle down on a record in the other room, whereafter jarringly harsh and gleeful *blatnyak* thieves' music echoed throughout the space. Vasya later remarked that upon hearing those heavenly sounds, it was as if a dove began fluttering in his breast, just like on the way back from the bird market when he was a very young boy. Such sweet pain comparable to a lover's first scratches, and yet, at the same time, another incredibly tragic element—a sense of life's last summer and the trickling of fresh, crystalline birch-resin tears—had erupted into the kitchen. Bully J. Badenov could vividly recollect every motion that followed. Enraptured, they waded to the source of the sounds, where they discovered the visitor had taken a guitar down off the wall, sat upon a table amidst heaped bottles of mineral water and cookie wrappers, and was now singing with his eyes squeezed shut. Oh, what freedom! What inexplicable *volyushka* issuing from a mouth opened only the width of a dash, as an eternal autobiographical minus sign, and delivered to the ears of the squatting listeners! A friendship was forged, the first records were cut, and before long, all the *militsiya* officers and their lovers in the little town were secretly playing on their mobile phones Arkasha's rendering of a song about two storks landing on the field outside a prison one night. And the officers wept as they fucked.

Arkady Dmitriyevich, or simply Arkasha, brushed crumbs from his saucer into his glazed teacup, stirred, and stared at the street through the swirling reflections and the shimmer off the windows. What he saw was not quite astral light, Paracelsus's *lux naturae*, the Hindus' *akasha*, the Chinese *qi*, or the Kabbalah Jewish *aor* . . . The morsels of cheap cake blending with the tea leaves in the brownish liquid were truly ignorant of the fact that even in the opening verses of the Gospel of John that had been written in ancient times, life and light were inseparably tied! To Arkasha, light was now more of a tool to prepare for suffering and survival. From the very moment he opened his eyes on the stairs every morning and lifted his head from the plastic bag, he'd have wished to close them again immediately, because still buzzing in his head were those foolish phrases and melodies that he'd played the previous night at the Rainbow lake restaurant. Occasionally, after the restaurant manager had gone home to bed, his friends and fellow musicians would allow him to sing his underground repertoire. The administrator would sigh and make weak threats, but even so, he didn't care much, because the Armenians would request the same song ten times in a row anyway and he'd pocket a shiny ruble afterward, too. On such nights, Arkasha would dazzle on the restaurant stage like the bachelors' sun or moon, or like an exotic pineapple amidst ultra-Stalinist Empire style, performing to tables of revelers who were mostly out of their heads already and staggering due to the rocking waves of the lake, due to the hooch they'd guzzled, due to storms on the sea of life.

All kinds of rumors about Arkasha circulated in the new, multicultural Viljandi: that he'd languished in jail for a long time (he'd only ever been held overnight in the drunk tank!), that he was the lovechild of a high-level Soviet-era communist, that he had come from Odessa but fell to drinking and lost his debit card, etc. Arkasha himself would lubricate such legends whenever he blabbed between caviar and champagne about having once been a pilot in Vietnam or having watched the world-famous film *The Godfather* in the company of its director while staying at the Ritz Hotel on a trip to Paris during the centenary of the most recent Republic of Estonia. Once, while arguing with a chubby CEO who wanted to pay to request a song, he even declared that chains, not a six-string guitar, were what really sung—and ripped the gold chain right off the insolent lard-face's neck! Arkasha had picked up a wealth of disgusting expressions from Konstantin Opiatovich when the pickpocket occasionally entered through the back room of the bookstore, bringing cognac with him. Overall, Arkasha truly behaved like an immortal *blatnoi-stilyaga*-jazzman. Before long, all the criminals of Viljandi proudly boasted of someone had been imprisoned with little Arkasha and what gleeful events had transpired. Konstantin Opiatovich, who knew all and was ever-informed of everything, observed these developments with a growing sense of unease—he was a logical man and knew it might all end poorly.

Osmo Vanska

Through his glass teacup, Arkasha spotted a very genteel-looking gentleman whose flushed face and gold-buttoned suit coat were pretentiously reflected in his patent leather shoes as he approached the bookstore. The man plodded along with a gentle hunch and abruptly ducked in through the door of a budget hostel. He reappeared a moment later, glaring around at his surroundings with a disgruntled expression.

Arkasha directed Bully J.'s attention to the unfamiliar seeker and entryway-enterer with a nod.

"Look, it's the great conductor, Vanska. What is he . . . drunk?"

Badenov looked over his shoulder and shook his head.

"Come on, that's not Vanska!"

"It sure is, look closer! It's that millionaire-*stilyaga*-producer Osmo Vanska, I'm sure of it!"

Badenov looked over his shoulder again and shook his head sharply.

"Arkasha, quit it . . ."

The individual passed the seated men with a conductor's sway in his step and tugged at the door to the puppet theater. A tuning fork was poking out of his pocket, in any event. The man was obviously looking for the pricy Hotel London, a red-brick building just ahead, on the corner of Castle and Post Streets. Arkasha stood up and called out:

"Mister maestro! Mister Osmo!"

Thereafter, things moved rapidly. The gentleman stopped in his tracks and stared at the men in surprise, puckering his lips and furrowing his brow. Arkasha didn't abandon hope.

"Pardon me, mister maestro, but your Sibelius performance was wonderful—truly the most outstanding gold-mask designer-chic!"

Flattered, the maestro bowed and snatched at the air as if grabbing ahold of a divine, invisible drainpipe. Then, he tiptoed onward at a snail's pace, this time heading straight for the hotel.

Arkasha hooted in laughter and jubilantly drained his cheap teacup filled with astral light. He'd been correct! Badenov was struck speechless. Great History itself had been here on this wretched street today, staggering past cigarette butts and addressing them personally! The conductor Osmo Vanska in person! Oh, that Arkasha of ours!

Noelhard Spring

The sales room of the used bookstore named Bookstore resembled, in certain respects, Badenov's communal room on the floor above. Whereas Bully J.'s walls were thick with vinyl records and band posters, here the intellectual partitions were crammed with emissaries of the enchanted kingdom of books, rather than representatives of the music world. The black-and-white tiled shop stocked with literary wares was made up of two cramped rooms. These were nearly identical except for the fact that in the first, nestled between the towering bookshelves, there was a revolving leather office chair with a cross-stitched back pillow with a picture of an owl on it, behind a desk on which rested a laptop and a cash register eagerly awaiting customers. Positioned at the focal point of the back room was a café table around which mostly local boys gathered to chat. Also stored in the rear were firewood and a tall ladder used to fetch top-shelf books or logs, according to need. Bars had been installed over the courtyard window during Estonian rule of the country, as a cellar bar that serviced relatively problematic customers had operated there. Ownership of the bookstore was somewhat obscure, but the legendary Noelhard Spring generally managed its affairs. He was best known for his van decorated with decals of crossed skeleton keys and Viljandi's suspension bridge, from which he offered key duplication services on Market Square. True, Noelhard did always have a few books on hand in the vehicle (works on the occult in particular), but they were primarily meant to lubricate his sales of shungite healing stones. It also never hurt to show potential buyers complex pyramid diagrams that visually demonstrated how a chunk of mysterious black Karelian mineraloid is capable of purifying up to 40,000 cubic meters of water! Noelhard's business plan was a stroke of genius, as every keyholder had to wait a few minutes while the machine chiseled in the grooves. It was during this precious interval that he occasionally managed to pawn off a stone using his diagrams, or if nothing else, then a keyring in the shape of a tiny shungite pyramid.

At the moment, however, Noelhard the *bouquiniste-zamok* maker-esoteric was poring over the ledgers. His mood was akin to that of a surrendered bar-cupboard key, because the assets and liabilities of the last few months unmistakably pointed to him having to use his retirement funds to make ends meet at the bookstore once again. Not even the amount necessary to cover the monthly card terminal fee had appeared in the credit column. The cash register was quite empty, popular interest in books had dwindled to almost nothing, and he reckoned that soon, he might as well start shoveling works from the high shelves into the oven instead of firewood. There were several reasons behind this drastic decline in sales. First of all, Noelhard was enraged by the secondhand shops from which one could haul home a wheelbarrow of literature for next to nothing. It had been ages since his firewood expenses could be covered by the intermittent sums accrued from selling forged Wiiralt sketches to tourists from the capital and beer and tea sales at the shop. Even Badenov and his Arkasha, not to mention many others, purchased potables more readily than books. What truly made his blood boil, however, were the tape decks and cassette players driving out classic vinyl players. The lucrative business he ran underground (or, rather, *upstairs* in Bully J. Badenov's communal room), which involved records cut on old X-ray films, had similarly started to dry up. Before, all he had to do was roll twenty or so of the soft records into his coat sleeve and stand outside the local hotel, after a few hours of which he could live carefree for a month or two. He would pick out a random yokel who'd ambled into town, his arms burdened with cakes and new boots, and would whisper conspiratorially into his ear, asking if he would like some Beatles or banned Estonian music. It went without saying that yes, the yokel would. Arkasha's Russian romances were a big hit in particular, and were eagerly scooped up by newcomers to the neighborhoods recently constructed

on the outskirts of town, among whose population
Arkasha's émigré laments evoked an all-too-bitterly-
cold sense of recognition. Noelhard would resolve any
problems involving the occasional profiteer-competitor-
record seller using a rather common method of force,
once even driving his key-making van over the toes
of one presumptuous "sleeve" (the nickname given to
such profiteering peddlers). The victim suffered such
an unfortunate fall through a diner window that he
ended up pulling the flashing neon hot-dog sign right
down onto his head by the wires! Noelhard despised the
sullying of the market—competitors/sleeves/*biznezmen*
would sometimes hawk records that played only four-
teen seconds of foul swearing that terminated in an
expressive cough. That was no way to behave. What's
more, the swindlers had started replacing the song lists
at the center of the record with pornographic images,
which Noelhard found unspeakably vulgar. Alas, the
old man was powerless in the face of the revolutionary
advent of all kinds of cassette players—the measures
of force he employed at the vegetable market were no
match against the cooperative department store, and he
couldn't just drive his key-making van over the polished
toenails of its entire female staff. Noelhard's situation
with women was already . . . complicated. He'd simply
failed to take a wife at the right moment! Nevertheless,
Noelhard didn't let his head hang, even though he knew
nothing short of a miracle could save the bookstore/
café. He'd already put too much work into it in his
younger days. He could walk blindfolded up to a shelf

and pull down any desired title . Everything was organized according to a strict system and a woman would only wreak havoc in the place! Placed directly in front of the cash register were thinner crime novels and boxes of postcards that were organized by country and city with cardboard dividing strips. Pricier military-themed postcards and old but unused congratulations and greetings cards were kept separate. Then, still within arm's reach, there was a photo album containing blurry home-printed band pictures and two albums of coins. Customers from the new suburbs would often inspect one of them with particular interest—it contained the kroon formerly used by the Estonians' lost democratic state and also euros, which briefly went into circulation not long before the regime change. Behind Noelhard's desk were the fishing and hunting sections and an exceptional specimen of foreign exoticism: one shelf stocked with copies of *National Geographic*—a bizarre magazine featuring unbelievable photographs. War veterans who came to purchase the magazine regarded it as a first-rate example of influential late-imperialist Western propaganda. Classic literature—Gogol, Dostoyevsky, and the other greats—was displayed in a place of honor directly above the *National Geographic* shelf, though most customers just bought cheap Russian-language fengshui pamphlets. Next to those, in turn, was a long shelf of nature works, beneath which was kept the shop's full collection children's literature. On the opposite wall, to the left of the window, were Western prose and historical works—at least as many titles as were permitted according to the strict state-issued lists. However, since Noelhard had acquired, sometime around the regime change, a store across the street that sold new books, he still possessed a relatively large collection of high-quality titles that had been published in free Estonia but which were now, according to the current ideology, quite obviously deemed unsuitable. These were stashed behind the English-language literature, which generally no one apart from Badenov and Vasya ever browsed. In the back room were the books with which Noelhard didn't very much wish to part—predominantly works on the occult, alongside art and photography albums, but also vinyl records, a coffee vending machine, and a beer-stocked refrigerator. Particularly vital to the old men, however, was the small toilet where Arkasha enjoyed reading Russian-language children's books.

Vasya Kolyugin

The Beatles maniac-Help!er-temple builder Vasya Kolyugin loudly proclaimed his usual "*all-yew-need-iz-laav*" to Arkasha and Badenov and breezed straight into the back room of the bookstore, because today, he'd brought along six small scale-model temples for sale. As Vasya was a trained sculptor, he'd made probably several hundred of them over the years, and in a wide range of sizes. The largest of them stood on his kitchen table at home, several meters tall and extending to the ceiling of the small, windowless room. According to his explanation, the model represented a nine-story cliff, at the foot of which was moored a yellow submarine-shaped aircraft, always ready for take-off, waiting to deliver visitors to their desired floor. His apartment, which was accessible from the alleyway next to the bookstore, did indeed resemble a museum dedicated to The Beatles or that submarine itself. Vasya had hung plaster reliefs of the band members directly above the thick metal door. By pressing the buzzer, a caller would naturally hear . . . the tune of Lennon's "Imagine"!

"*Gaad bless yew!*" Vasya yelled to Noelhard, who was presently working on forging Wiiralt's signature in the lower margin of a photocopied drawing that depicted a wrinkly old Berber man. There seemed to be no other escape from bankruptcy.

"If only God willed it," sighed Noelhard. Vasya swept the ledgers off the table and laid his temple models in their place.

"What are you all worried about?"

"Vasya," Noelhard began stridently. Yet, realizing his woes wouldn't be understood anyway, resigned himself to picking up the ledgers and placing them on a shelf next to a French-language book about Tutankhamun's tomb, which had been there since the days of the Estonian Republic.

"Precisely! Disarray is holy, but when disarray becomes holiness, then it's all just disarray!" Vasya remarked, patting the smallest of the temples absentmindedly. He was able to marvel endlessly at his own craftsmanship, because he was guided by the spirit of Lennon!

"Let me tell you—Lennon himself will come and check out our temple, you'll see! I've got it all worked out. Look, there are nine stories, each thirty feet high. On each floor, people will lie there for four minutes listening to *all-yew-need-is-laav*—total bliss, you'll see—and ride the submarine from floor to floor."

Vasya gazed affectionately at the model as if waiting for the matchbook-sized clay submarine to take flight.

"All this accounting and book-cooking is driving me to despair!" Noelhard interrupted wearily.

"Take it easy, Noelhard." Vasya glanced at the sketch of the desert dweller. "Why aren't you selling any Beatles pictures here? Where's Lennon? You know, man, I went to go see an old friend once—he was a big Beatles fan back in the day, but no matter how hard I looked, I couldn't find a single Beatles picture hanging on his walls! Just crystal everywhere you looked. Crystal, you get me?! Crystal! His wife, Lyubochka, right? she wouldn't allow it, he told me . . . Hey, you want me to bring you a Lennon?"

Noelhard didn't. He scowled apprehensively at the almost fully depleted stack of firewood next to the bookshelf reserved for drama. Someone had jabbed an old broken umbrella between the logs.

Vasya snorted. "Yeah, ladies don't like The Beatles —just crystal. They're sweet for cash, even though all they do is talk about love. In reality, they don't know a single thing about it. Only John did! Let me ask you: why can't you build anything with just love? Huh? I'd have had the temple ready ages ago! Who's to blame? Money alone, I tell you—money . . ."

Noelhard still looked rather concerned.

"But Noelhard, dear," Vasya continued, "something should be done about it, then. Say we throw together an old-school home concert. You remember? Just like back in the day. Everybody paid a euro and waited all scared-like for the *militsiya* to show up—the Estonian police, I mean. All the collectors got together—all the old jazz prisoners; the relapse music-lovers. *Tikett-to-rayd*, man! First, we listened to music; afterward, we drank tea. What a high! Or how 'bout this— what if we all go about building this temple together now, hey? Grab the temple by the horns? I was thinking that we could have one gate face Mommy Russia and the other look westward. I'm telling you; you know?! We'll welcome Lennon there with tears in our eyes! All of America will curtsy to us! It'll be a *vechnoe* high!"

"I suppose we really must do something about it," murmured Noelhard, pulling the umbrella out of the firewood stack. It was ancient and probably worth donating to a museum.

"He-he-he—do you remember when the police came and poked around my room that was all covered in Beatles stuff? Where music and love spurted like a fountain? Rock and roll really is the social avant-garde!"

Vasya patted Noelhard on the shoulder and pushed a little temple model in front of him.

"Now imagine this temple of love, right?! You could listen to the Beatles there; could send the world your prayers, so to say. The Beatles *are* angels, right?! God's envoys; pure love! You know, the Estonian Republic was what it was back in the day, but *I'm* not going to spit on the tsardom, either. You know how much I've walked the corridors of the Governorate of Estonia talking about renaming a street for Lennon?! Take this

one—Castle Street. Come on! They laugh. They'd rather
have everybody pull on overcoats, not jeans! All in all,
this whole tsardom is just like that friend's apartment—
everywhere you look, it's just crystal, women, nature,
bears, and then crystal again."

The tiny temple of mercy glowed in the middle of
the room, as Vasya had lit the cheapest tea candle he
could find there. Enclosed by tall bookshelves and old
flower-print wallpaper, the space was filled with the
flickering sense of your already standing on a floor of
that envisioned temple. Nevertheless, Noelhard shook
himself out of the reverie—some idiot had stacked all
the black-bound Estonian-era encyclopedias in a pre-
carious tower atop a cupboard that was starting to tilt
threateningly! Mundane tasks were in dire need of
attention.

The bookstore door suddenly swung open with a
jingle. Noelhard rushed out of the backroom.

"Oh, it's you two," he sighed disappointedly when
he saw it was just Badenov and Arkasha.

"You've no idea what Arkasha just pulled off! He
startled Vanska! Maestro Osmo!"

Bemused, Noelhard looked over at Arkady, whose
face was drawn into an ear-to-ear grin like that of a
jack-o'-lantern samovar. A thought abruptly came to
his mind and, mumbling to himself, he took the cal-
endar off the wall. He was right: the date was circled in
thick red marker, which meant the bookstore's monthly
cultural discussion evening. Penciled beneath the number was today's topic: "The Practice and Theory of Love

Throughout the Ages". The new town government supported such types of educational undertaking, but unfortunately, Noelhard had been given his entire yearly stipend in advance and had immediately spent it all on winter tires for the van. Arkasha attempted to duck out, but Badenov locked the door and tossed the key to Noelhard.

"I believe we will now retire for discussion," Noelhard sighed, his eyes wearily rolling back in their sockets. Not that he was in any particular mood for it, of course, but governorate inspectors might show up, in principle, as the lecture times had been forwarded to them and adherence to the schedule was mandatory.

Peladan McCartneyvich Plato

You could say the tradition of Noelhard's esoteric evenings had withstood every regime within memory. He had acquired an introductory knowledge of the occult from members of the Metapsyche Club in the days of the first Republic of Estonia, and from their legendary officer Joonas Fail, in particular. In truth, all the locals in the field (even the astrologists, tarot readers, and others of that ilk) had once learned the basics from that spry old gentleman when he lived right there in Viljandi. It was no wonder that Noelhard kept the books he'd inherited from Fail in the tiny back room of the shop and refused to sell them for any price. In time, the other students had all gained fame in their respective fields and had forgotten their teacher, but not Noelhard. He had dealt mainly in tarot and birthday cards during the Soviet period, ran a small astrological bookstore named The Sky Is Open in a former lingerie store during the fleeting era of the restored Republic of Estonia, and had ultimately retreated into the back room of the used bookstore as if into an intellectual trench due to the conditions enforced by the new tsardom. In preparation for the day's discussion, Noelhard had already scoped out the primary romance titles to use as ammunition. Arkasha was reading a Czech children's book (not a word of which he could understand) on the toilet and had left the door open a crack. Today's romance-themed discussion intrigued him—it wouldn't simply be water off a duck's back, as it would be nice to use the quotations and examples to show off and win hearts at the Rainbow later. His own marriage had unfortunately ended as swiftly as a tennis endgame when his wife realized how utterly incompetent her husband was at bringing in income. She tried to support Arkasha for a little while longer, as if he were a plastic singing doll, but ultimately gave up, handed him a plastic bag of clean underclothes, and threw him out.

Noelhard began the meeting with the customary porridge lines from Hauff's fairy tale "Little Muck": "Hither, come hither! The porridge is here; The table I've spread, Come taste of my cheer. Your neighbors bring with you, um . . . come fast, I've made lots of porridge." Noelhard cherished ceremonies, and that mysterious little passage had served him loyally for decades! He lit a candle before a picture of his guru and began.

"Love can be viewed from either a neo-Platonic or a Christian standpoint. To the former, it is erotic energy and a natural foundation; Eros, so to say; private emotion. To the latter, conversely, it is the struggle against sin; the love/suffering/ascetic."

A roll of toilet paper bounced across the floor from Arkasha's direction. Badenov gently rolled it back. Giggling came from within. "But there is still a third way, you know!" Vasya interrupted. "The Beatles' way; John's way!"

"Vasya, there have always been attempts made to combine both approaches, but what we must understand is that the sexual relationship in an ordinary family is merely a banal shadow compared to what actually lies within," continued Noelhard, unflustered.

"Yeah, keep that in mind, Vasya," someone murmured in a low, holy voice. Arkasha peeked out from behind the door, his mouth full of toilet paper.

"What truly matters is neither reproduction nor satisfaction, but the metaphysical conjunction of the sexes—the striving toward wholeness on a higher level!" Noelhard cast a troubled glance towards the toilet, whence odd noises were coming. "However, in order to fulfill this lofty task, the man must become even more masculine and the woman even more feminine—ultimately, they should converge in the Androgyne. Alas, every social disturbance gives rise to pointless sexual passions; to a sex-pandemic; to gynecocracy. Man is perpetually aroused, psychologically agitated, and thus, will not arrive at that sacred plane."

Noelhard took a thick book stamped *Mahanirvana Tantra* in gold lettering out of a box and read from it aloud: "When men have become subject to women and slaves of lust, oppressors of their friends and Gurus, then know that the Kali Age has become strong."

Arkasha had meanwhile quieted down in his nook. Just then, however, the end of a roll of toilet paper, with something written upon it, was pushed beneath the door. Badenov noticed the scribbled paper snake and began discreetly pulling it towards himself with his foot.

Vasya had been listening tranquilly as he fondly watched the tea candle flicker in the temple model. Suddenly, he stirred.

"I agree! Love shapes man and history—it's all you need! But if you marry a lady named Lyuba and all she does is buy crystal and doesn't even let you hang John's picture on the wall, then the only choice you have is to escape. All the great gods support passion and love— just look at Indians' Kali or The Beatles' John!"

Badenov felt he had to speak up as well. He'd been hoping to be left in peace for a little while so he could study what words of genius Arkasha had scrawled on the toilet paper. It was apparently a statement in verse. Unfortunately, nothing to say came to mind.

"The supra-physical subtle body is the substrate of gender—a transition between the material and the immaterial. Love is indeed like the synergy of two fantasies; like gender magic. Even in the Upanishads, it's written that the goal of a man and woman's striving is not simply love, but total immortality; all-encompassing light; atman! An example from Western culture could be the Fideli d'Amore movement, which interpreted the word *amor* as *a-mors*, meaning "without death." Ordinary gods do not like such human activity, naturally—the androgyne always endangers the divine. It is a dangerous path, or as Eschenbach says in *Parzival*: "The path to the Holy Grail reveals itself to man only with weapon in hand!'"

Noelhard had worked himself up into a frenzy and seemed to be debating with himself.

"At the same time, Plato says that reproduction and birth *are* the manifestations of immortality in a mortal being!"

"There's an icon of Plato in a church in the Kremlin. His remains are said to have been baptized there," Badenov finally piped up. He grunted matter-of-factly and, with one sharp tug, pulled out the entire length toilet paper to study it more closely. Inside the toilet, Arkasha was singing in bizarre Czech baby-talk.

"You're absolutely correct. Whereas the great Plato compared love to a fever, Bourget in his modern-love psychology asserts that a lover who seeks anything other than love itself within love—in order to gain profit or respect, for instance—is no longer a lover. Rather, that love is a surrogate; a tremendous failure!"

Noelhard removed several dustier books from his crate of ammunition.

"Even Péladan in his love/science masterpiece emphasizes that realism in love is no less absurd than realism in art. He says that life's hierarchies simply find realism repugnant! A totally distinct field of study within this topic is love in dreams—here, Piobb is the authority and uncrowned king with his magical work on Venus, in which he studied why ejaculation during sleep is often even more powerful than in waking life, and is even observed among the crippled and the elderly!"

To Badenov's disappointment, Arkasha had merely written another filthy *Poruchik* Rzhevsky joke about Natasha Rostova and saddled horses. Vasya was still mesmerized by the candle in the temple model.

"So, you can only draw conclusions about women if you compare them to absolute femininity and men to absolute masculinity. It is the substrate of gender— *sukshma sarira* to the Hindus and the heavenly body to Paracelsus. In every era, wise men have known that androgyny alone can lead to immortality, because the embryo itself is initially an epicene! Yet, Eros frequently comes demanding his own, and everything surrounding that romance is wrecked and destroyed in the process . . ."

"I'm not sure these things are really so complicated," Vasya said with a dismissive wave. "I'd just say *long-livv-rockenroll* and Beatles forever! I bet these scholars of yours just haven't looked into the right guys. Take McCartney, for instance—the man's a god, but he went on stage once in Leningrad, tripped, and cried out *Privet rebyata!* in Russian! Do you understand? Now *that's* class! Sanya just shimmied up a lamppost on Palace Square and yelled: free, free-e-e! There's nothing more to say."

"The Beatles, androgynes, Palace Square . . . this really is an awful drama," Arkasha interjected through the doorway, which he opened a crack. "Gentlemen, let me ask: have you ever had vinaigrette thrown on you at a restaurant? I'm talking about vinaigrette right on your bare back! Once, I was kissing a lady at the Rainbow. The fountain was already covered in flowers, so to say, I'd just taken off my shirt, and then, her husband, I guess, that asshole—he came out of the men's room, saw me, and flung a stranger's bowl of vinaigrette at my back as hard as he could!"

Everyone laughed. Noelhard realized the lecture was probably over for that day and began sullenly returning the books to the ammunition crate. Arkasha was still on a roll.

"Luckily, it was a glass bowl—if it'd been Czech crystal, then . . . The thing with women is, right, like it goes in that song: you don't erect a monument on a square to just any of them or put their faces on a coin, but they all want to ride in a taxi, pretty and ugly alike. You go walking with some of them like a widow with a pioneer and you see that, well, there's nothing to see! But the *attraction*, fuck! The attraction's just oy-oy-oy like an April in Paris, you know? Better watch your back!"

Badenov and Vasya whinnied in laughter while Arkasha scaled the ladder to the ceiling like a sniper mounting a slender mother birch.

"Hey, Arkady—we're still on serious topics here. Love and music are sacred," Vasya said reproachfully, amid his laughter.

"I'm just telling it the way it is," crowed Arkasha in a high-pitched baby's voice from behind the chandelier.

Suddenly, Konstantin Opiatovich was standing in the middle of the room amidst all that gleeful melancholy. He'd apparently picked the lock, because the key still rested securely in the breast pocket of Noelhard's checkered shirt. Yet, the pickpocket hadn't come alone. He was accompanied by a sharp-nosed stranger with sunken cheeks who was wrapped entirely in a brown shroud. Visibly electrified, Opiatovich hurried to fetch a chair from next to the wall and with the deepest respect helped the visitor seat himself. Then, he carefully set a bulging wallet on the man's lap. The ghostly guest coughed at length and then mumbled something indistinct. His voice seemed to emerge from deep underground.

"Place your hands on the oven . . . is what was always done . . . when the dead were seen . . ."

Opiatovich carefully removed an old-fashioned large-format calling card from the wallet and ceremoniously handed it to Noelhard. He then wiped sweat from his brow with a handkerchief; his face was glowing like a burning bush.

"Nikolai Vasilievich Gogol!"

"Konstantin Opiatovich, please just call me Mikola as we agreed. Simply Mikola will do . . . for the dead, so to speak . . ."

There was a crash. Arkasha had tumbled from the ladder and now lay next to the umbrella and the last remaining firewood. The stack of teetering encyclopedias tenderly covered his scrawny, confused body like the first delicate snowfall settling upon a puppy playing in a basket.

Natasha and Petrusha

Dreaming is a fine pastime when all the right conditions have been met! In the interests of authenticity, the Viljandi Imperial Civic Museum had not been hooked up to the electrical grid. Nevertheless, the nineteenth century, in which the exhibition and the fetching young researcher named Natasha both strove to immerse themselves with all their might, hung suspended in the air of the museum not because of the lack of ceiling lights, but as a direct result of the old receptionist Zinaida Prokofyevna. Born during the Siege of Leningrad and having survived the Siege of Tallinn seventy years later, the elderly woman would play solitaire on the samovar table in the main hall every morning. Natasha sometimes wondered whether solitaire could be regarded as a game at all, because if you compared what Zinaida did to soccer, for example, then there were certainly no similarities to be found between the two. Occasionally, the woman would doze off at her card game and be so genuinely still that visitors took her for a waxwork. Natasha had also remarked Zinaida's uncanny likeness to a portrait that hung over the Biedermeier sofa, which the museum had received from a former shelter for noblewomen. Zinaida Prokofyevna's resemblance to the sensual, unknown Baltic German baroness was especially magical at sunset when reddish rays of light danced upon the candlestick and the large samovar on the table, making it seem as if a mirror were hanging on the wall. An attentive observer would, of course, notice that whereas the Baltic dame wore an autumn-brown cameo brooch, Zinaida Prokofyevna had two medals pinned to her chest, presented to her for surviving the blockades, one with an image of Lenin, the other with the profile of the current tsar. Natasha was eternally grateful to the wise governorate for having appointed Zinaida as her assistant, because at night, when the time came to blow out the candles and lock the door of the apartment museum, it would have been some-what unnerving to walk through the darkened rooms to the exit alone. The tiny office next to the kitchen where Natasha worked on her research was cozy, of course, but . . . even in the kitchen, with its fishtail-patterned brick floor and strange old elegant Estonian copper dishes glinting in the cabinets, the imposing silence that pressed its way into every nook and cranny would knock the wind out of her. The apartment was so unlike her dormitory room on Pine Hill!

Natasha was compiling a *sbornik* of 1,500 Russian adages and their Estonian equivalents. The Russian portion of her doctoral work was grounded upon the masterpiece study by Dahl and Rybnikov, and for the Estonian section, she'd managed to find materials from the Museum of Estonian Literature's proverb archive, which had been miraculously preserved in the University of Tartu's administrative building despite the rest of the city being razed in the war. The tiny room packed with boxes of filing cards was located right next to a Russian Orthodox chapel—at first, some of the old sayings had felt so sacrilegious that she had wanted to pull a curtain between her and the wall of icons. Nevertheless, a sage professor and war veteran helped her to get over her initial mortification and now, the whole project ahead of her had been classified into clear and logical sections. Natasha divided the adages into the broad categories of temporal relationships, lives, human characteristics, man and community, man and work, property, societal and communal rules, ethical norms, and finally, folk philosophy. There were, of course, many adages that could be placed into multiple categories, such as the Estonian saying, "You can't fool an old sparrow with chaff," but her professor advised her not to delve too deep. Natasha was thrilled by the knowledge that different peoples had identical measures for good and evil, even in the case of cultures that had had absolutely no direct interaction. The Estonians, Russians, Persians, and even—oh my—the Japanese knew, for example, that, "A thick log takes a thick wedge." Most of all, however, Natasha was fond of the maxims on romance, which she would happily research for hours at a time.

Yet, as they say, "Your tongue will take you to Turkey, but your legs will lead you nowhere," and, "One little hour-long nap will lead to a lifelong trap!"

Sleep is for the dead, indeed! On this day, Natasha had to run to the governorate offices to fetch next year's budget form, to the market to buy good Estonian-baked barankas (as someone had bitten several in half, right off the nail they hung upon, while Zinaida Prokofyevna dozed), to the pet store to beg for birdseed (a deficit item) to feed the museum bedroom's parakeets, and where-all-else. Prior to these errands, however, she needed to update the exhibition by rotating out a few watercolor paintings by the dilettante Zdekauer from his collection "Viljandi Types"—a weekly activity. At first, Natasha had been astounded by the kinds of clothes people used to wear! Coats with sleeves that drooped to the ground, visored karakul hats, and particularly one image of a snobbish man wearing a hat with earflaps that resembled a giant cloth snail shell! Whenever she found a moment to herself, she could be seen taking a breath of fresh air on the museum balcony or digging in the courtyard, where there was a small herb garden in need of motherly care. There's no point in closing the gate after the horse has bolted! And, of course, we must not forget her essential nightly dancing in a circle around the Market Square fountain, which depicted a boy with a fish; or her frantic sprints through the chilly summer night onto the last, romantically droning, metro train . . . Oh, Saint Alexander Nevsky, how suffocatingly beautiful this old Estonian dolls' town of Viljandi was!

Quarreling echoed from the entryway.

"I will not permit you to see Natasha!"

Oh, Saint Mary of Egypt! Zinaida Prokofyevna was arguing with that dreadful artist Petrusha! Yet again! The renowned cuckoo had come asking for her just yesterday! Today, too!?

"Huh?" Petrusha drawled with the incredulity of a fool. "And who do you think you are to forbid me to visit Natasha? Perhaps I'd like to buy a ticket? To see the exhibition?"

Zinaida Prokofyevna didn't back down. Petrusha chewed his lip and tossed the butt of a filterless *papirosa* cigarette into the umbrella bin.

"Listen, you old hag—maybe I'm about to get married! Maybe my bride is the Princess of Sarajevo! Maybe my new family calls me the Viking of the North! Maybe I just want to observe your Biedermeier for a while, to see how I'll furnish my future castle more nobly!"

"Viking of the North?" Zinaida Prokofyevna echoed with a cruel cackle. "All you are is a famous dysgraphic piss-your-pants *nemodny*! Don't you remember how you wrote 'pus shit' instead of 'bus sheet' on the wall newspaper at school? Huh? Should I remind you?"

Natasha hurried to intervene. She gave Zinaida a soothing pat on the shoulder and timidly beckoned Petrusha into the farthest room in the museum—the one with the birdcage. She didn't love the young man, but she did feel sorry for him. What's more, no one is safe when they suddenly find themselves in the claws of their former grade-school cleaning woman . . . Zinaida

Prokofyevna glared at the two as they walked away, then nipped into the kitchen for a cup of tea. All the while, she kept a close eye on the silverware.

"Just try living with folks like these!" she grumbled to herself. "And you've got no Leningrad or Hermitage here, either. Where have all the proper folk gone? It's as if they were annihilated; as if were swallowed up by the metro!"

"I'm not respected here. Not one tiny bit," Petrusha sighed to the parrots in the cage as he sat down on the creaking antique bed. Natasha considered fetching tea from the kitchen, but changed her mind as she didn't want to irritate Zinaida Prokofyevna any further.

"You should paint more—people's appreciation will certainly grow then," the blushing Natasha reassured the young man as she took a seat on the watchwoman's chair in the opposite corner of the room. Petrusha's pant legs had ridden up unattractively and it was obvious he wasn't wearing socks with his sandals.

"No, Natashka—I will never achieve fame in this town!" he declared, casting a sorrowful look at his unwashed toes. "But I can tell you this: today, on the tram, I believe I glimpsed an even more unfortunate soul than I. The poor man was dressed in rags and even despite that, he was *still* being stalked by that old pickpocket Konstantin! The moment I saw that riffraff, my thoughts immediately went to your . . . that is, to *my* miserable state . . ."

"Miserable state," Natasha echoed, then dodged the dangerous topic by steering the conversation toward the parrot cage. "You did have your own school here in Viljandi—that . . . shadow-people movement?"

What a miserable man this Petrusha really is, Natasha thought. Ragged pants; the cheapest sandals imaginable; an odd, clinging smell of smoke probably caused by a cracked wood-heated stove somewhere in the dreary suburb called Kantreküla, where the air was always choked with rustic gray chimney smoke. Even so, didn't the young man's expression possess something elusively aristocratic, ironical, condescending? The whole town was familiar with his pitiful tale. In the waning years of the true Estonian democracy, the country had experienced a bizarre and inexplicable economic boom, during which many had borrowed beyond their means. Petrusha had likewise mortgaged his dear lakeside house (which cars crashed into every year after failing to take the curve down the hill) and taken out a loan to buy a quaint manor just outside of town. Alas, the dramatic imperial economic depression had flung the young castellan into the jaws of bankruptcy! A buyer was found for the manor, but the little house could no longer be sold at such a good price. Although the new tsardom did write off all earlier loans within just a couple of years, their numbers dispersing like smoke in the sky and freeing borrowers of financial obligations in a single day thanks to the tsar's wise ukase, there was also one incredibly negative turn of events. Namely, a legal descendant of the last Volga German to occupy the manor house (the man's great-grandchild) surfaced from the depths of Siberia and demanded what was rightfully his. This repeated crashing of fate's piano lid affected Petrusha's mental interior and his physical exterior like a grating wrong note.

"You see? Even *you* can't remember correctly, even though you attended our final exhibition at the train station—our school was called the Society of the Dark Side." Petrusha's gaze drilled angrily into the fattened caged birds. Ticking away somberly in a nest-shaped wooden watch-holder on the wall was a grand nine-teenth-century pocket watch that had once belonged to the legendary mayor Maramantchik. Petrusha despised everything in the room—apart from the museum researcher, of course.

Natasha glanced furtively at the watch, then at the birdcage. She hadn't bought the birdfeed yet! The hour was already so late! She did, of course, remember the exhibition held years ago, at which she had foolishly ended up in the company of her good friend who taught art at the Viljandi Lyceum for Girls. Morbid paintings in frighteningly dark tones, which were hung in the bare, high-ceilinged train station. Each displayed the exact same motif and a repetitive obsession: a grim-faced woman in a long dress holding a lantern and star-ing into the distance in front of that very train station at midnight. And the young, troubled artist's long and embarrassing opening speech in the empty waiting hall, the guiding theme of which was his absurd outlook on life: the more he painted, the more greatly he suffered, and yet, there was no other way. Terrible!

"I really must go now! Honestly, I must!" Natasha

blurted loudly and to her own surprise. With words, you will cross the Volga; with acts, not even the strait to Saaremaa!

Footsteps immediately shuffled away from the door, which had been left slightly ajar, into the darkness of the entryway.

Petrusha's Little Lights

Petrusha fled down the stairs like a sleepwalker. Away, away from here! What had he even hoped for . . . The strange sensation that overcame him like a fever when he saw the odd couple of the pickpocket and his victim on the tram; the conviction that he had to see Natasha at once, and all would be miraculously resolved—once again, it had been a deception. His wits in utter disarray, Petrusha turned down an alleyway. Moonlight illuminated an inner courtyard lined by tall, narrow windows; ghostly old floorless balconies sneered at him in a French sort of way, like Napoleon, like centuries. In an intrinsically Estonian fashion, the barred and padlocked ground-floor iron shop doors led nowhere. Only one doorway cast a narrow ribbon of light into the night. Seeing nothing, hearing nothing, Petrusha stumbled towards the weak glow as if traversing the field of life, but then tired of the distant promise and staggered, defeated, back onto the main street, simply and ultimately to go home.

Poetically, one could probably say that Petrusha's dreams had not quite fully seeped through the foul reek of smoke that insidiously seeped from the Russian stove into the charming apartment in the moonlight-bathed wooden Kantreküla house. Petrusha liked his suburban rental—the railroad delivered metropolitan excitement a couple times per day and reliable morning frost coated the patches of vomit and piss in the filthy stairwell. The eternal twilight of the slum, the distant barking of gaunt dogs, the musty smell of the torn wool blanket nailed over the stairwell door, the sun that only ever took half-dead steps—it always sweated, stunk, scratched its existence into the blood right here in his squalid little room; in the crack in the wooden floor beside the bed. Even so, the glow of sunset would sometimes scatter patches of golden light onto the narrow rat-gnawed floorboards like precious coins, reflected off the cross of the tiny Orthodox church nearby (formerly a morgue), and even appeared to nurture Petrusha. After the golden sunlight spilled across his floor, the sopping tarpaper of night no longer felt so low and oppressive. Alas, autumn winds always arrived as warm August came to an end and brought with them an inexplicable longing, as if someone had discarded a garland on the roadside amid an endless desolate steppe. Soon, the intoxicated trees beyond the railway tracks froze like weary drunks and only the feeble deceptive glow of the hazardous, faraway Glassmaker's Bar could be perceived through the biting, frigid blizzard. Nordic time was so fleeting—one could read by a summery window or marvel at a bird for no

more than a moment before the fishes' mouths began to
freeze in the rivers and the growling dogs could no longer tell whether you were friend or foe due to the cold,
and thus tended to snap at you indiscriminately. Once,
last winter, Petrusha had gone for a walk across a field
and Cold itself had spoken to him, whispering amid the
swirling snow that it longed to have him. Yet, Petrusha
mustered all his strength, got up, and reeled home like
a servant or a caretaker whose path has crossed his master's on an unpermitted amble. Lord Frost had ground
his frozen cigarette butt straight through Petrusha's torn
buttonhole, but he somehow made it home, regardless. Later, sitting in front of the fire, he realized that
his shoddy room with its wash jug and hard bed would
simply have been let out to the next identically unfortunate soul a week later, without any kind of emotion,
and the pain was like a black icon frame. Truly, nothing
in the world would have changed because of it—not
the slightest thing! Not until another spiritual drifter
crossed the railroad tracks in a blizzard one day and
met his end. Perhaps that man's final thoughts as he collapsed into Lord Frost's snowy ashtray would likewise
have been of a tiny bird flitting through a garden or a
book left on a windowsill.

Therefore, Petrusha did not put his fate to the test
just yet. What's more, the field beyond the railway
tracks was very far away. Dazed from the blow dealt
to his basket of love in the museum, he set off rather
mechanically for home.

Grigori Cuffovich Cuff

The guitarist-ignoramus-*kostyumchik* Grigori Cuffovich Cuff had been performing with Bully J. Badenov at the Rainbow lake restaurant for years. During their most recent season, however, Grigori Cuffovich had also provided musical accompaniment for evening programs at the Novel, a literary locale. It made no difference whether he played those songs while wearing a blue woolen track suit in his room on evenings off or dressed up in a slightly more formal brown suit coat and did the same-old, same-old for a handful of kopecks at the late-night venue. Today, he'd even shown up exceptionally early (by his standards) in order to have a go at doing a *kvakushka*, for the purposes of which he had a special little box with a pedal that could be used to summon surreal sounds from the guitar. Grigori Cuffovich had recently bought it from Badenov, who was permanently strapped for cash. It came as no surprise—all of Bully J.'s extra money was now spent on that Arkasha! Rumor had it he'd even gotten him a new suit! Naturally, at home, Grigori agonizingly had to explain to Lyuba why she wouldn't receive this month's crystal vase and bear painting, as well as why Badenov's musical tool was crucial to his daily work. Relations with his wife Lyuba had been poor for a very long time—it felt like his spouse only had enough passion for the consignment shop. After returning from her shopping trips, Lyuba would merely stare at her haul with a dull, adoring gaze; soften up for a split second; and by that same evening, already be addressing Grigori in her usual hostile tone. Luckily, Lyuba was unaware that this *kvakushka* device was no new invention; that all the great guitarists had used it in their day, performing the "baked chick" and the "frog" with the genius equipment on many an occasion; using the box to make their guitar "croak." If she'd known, then she probably wouldn't have let him buy it! Still, an implement like that was an unprecedented wonder in tiny Viljandi. Out of the blue and in dire financial straits, Badenov had knocked on Grigori's door and offered to sell him the magical device, having constructed the necessary connections out of a telephone cable and parts pulled from some geological instrument. A quick trial showed that the designer croak-effect really did have a mighty impact, and to Grigori's amazement, his old songs now sounded unbelievably modern. All he had to do was press down the little pedal with his tattered sock and "The Seagull of the Neva" became genuine Boney M! The Novel was frequented by a younger, more liberal crowd (mainly students from the local cultural institute), who went nuts for that kind of retro-*kvakushka* disco. Grigori Cuffovich had seemed to take on a new lease of life and had even accrued a few rather lissome admirers—pretty, devoted Novel *kvakushka-katyushas*! Just the other day, one such admirer had even spotted him at the intersection of Castle and Yuryev streets and had cried out in a cheerful, awfully loud voice: "Hey, Santana! Santana!" Such things really warmed your heart! An old woman in front of the ice cream stand who overheard the commotion crossed herself from right to left and frightenedly asked the retailer why on earth Orthodox youth would be summoning Satan . . .

Yes, Grigori's initial unease regarding the locale named Novel quickly passed. It certainly had no tablecloths, unlike at the Rainbow, and not even a host, but the guests were somehow friendlier and more interesting. Here, there were no dreadful watermelon sellers or seamen on shore leave like those who went to hit the bottle at the Rainbow. Nor were there any locals—only students, ever pretty and merry. Before long, Grigori could start picking out individual faces from the mass. Actors from the little local theater stood out first of all: the male ballet dancer who resembled a lanky stork, always ordered vodka and juice, and was the subject of all kinds of filthy whispered rumors; and the tragic actress who wore black fishnet gloves. Luckily, both ended up being three sheets to the wind relatively quickly and never came up to torture him with any song requests. Fishnet-glove-girl did once ask for a singer completely

unknown in the socialist camp—some Sinatra fellow—but instead, Grigori played the Chelyabinsk
band Ariel's song "Lyuli, Lyuli" while secretly using his
kvakushka pedal, and in the end, everyone was satisfied! Novel was an honest place; unlike the Rainbow,
where they cleverly employed red tablecloths to hide
the late-night bloodspray-from-the-boxer's-nose! Well,
and that Arkasha whom Badenov waited on hand and
foot—how was it that a *blatnoi-primitiv-muzykant* like
him was seen as a good artist, all of a sudden?! He was
uneducated! All he did was rasp, nothing more—he was
a dark unmusical element!

Fatty Mummies

Grigori entered the Novel via the kitchen, which is to say from the courtyard. Regular customers came in through the door that gave onto the park, but he had a nice little tradition whereby the exotic Estonian barwoman Katerina served him a glass of whipped cream and a shot of Kiiu Bashnya egg liqueur before he performed. The liqueur was actually used for their cake recipes, but . . . Today, the divine Katerina was busy. She placed an opened mini-bottle of liqueur before Grigori and hurried off to serve tables. Someone had ordered four of the day's specials! Grigori peered through a knothole in the wall, and—what do you know! It appeared there was an event underway for members of the local pensioners' club, The Silvery Silver Thread, to mingle, as there were only old men seated around two tables! Badenov and Arkasha were there, too! This certainly had to be investigated! That pair was rarely seen at the Novel.

Grigori Cuffovich took one of the plates and followed

Katerina out of the kitchen. Badenov gave him a solemn nod and pointed. All four plates were for some unfamiliar *stilyaga*! Presently, Arkasha was trying to direct his usual drivel at the stranger, who emptied one plate after another. He gasped as he dined in a highly unusual and inept manner, like a baby taking its first bites.

"Mister Gogol," Arkasha spoke, deferentially breaking the silence, "I'd like you to know that I've dined with other men of great fame before, too. Once, when I was in Sochi for an exhibition, Brezhnev himself invited me to join him at his table—that was in the seventies of last century, during the days of the Soviet Union. Leonid Ilyich, in person! He called me over and offered me, just imagine! Bulgarian yogurt. He was on vacation, wearing a mesh shirt, just like me."

Gogol cast a brief glance at Arkasha, who seized the opportunity to continue the story, which the others knew held zero credibility. Leaning against the back of Badenov's chair, Grigori bent down to softly ask what was going on. Badenov stared back in bemusement.

"Grigori Cuffovich, do you truly not recognize him? Or are you playing the *durak*?"

"Well, I'll be damned . . ." the guitarist murmured in astonishment, gazing at the writer whose portrait had once hung on the wall of his Moscow grade school, as he destroyed, in the here and now, Katerina's chicken Kiev special. *Gogol* . . .

Noelhard Spring emerged from the toilet and threatened Arkasha before he even reached the table. The rest of the men also started rebuking him. Gogol had finished off the last chicken Kiev and was now staring dully at the table in front of him, his belly full.

Noelhard wiped his brow with the back of his hand and devoutly declared: "Nikolai Vasilievich, we, the people of this small town, now have an unparalleled opportunity to ask you, an old-school classic: what is it like in the afterlife, i.e. in the world of the occult? And how would you describe the nature of love?"

Gogol ignored him completely, merely gripping the armrests of his chair more tightly. His hands were shriveled and dark, as if mummified.

"Mister Gogol, where are you going?"

The man spoken to had risen with difficulty and was crossing the room on his way to the toilet, wobbling as he went. The Novel was a compact place and the bathroom was raised half a floor, accessed via narrow steps leading to a balcony near the counter. The classic-*viy*-mummy seized the banister with both hands as he climbed the stairs; a strip of fabric slipped off his back and trailed behind him, finally to poke out from under the closed door like the end of a roll of toilet paper.

"What does it matter to you, Noelhard? And, by the way, which one of you is paying?" snapped Katerina, who had been listening in on the men's prattle from behind the bar with only lukewarm interest. Luckily, no other customers had arrived yet. As soon as the toilet door was latched shut, great passions burst forth in the little Novel.

"The Beatles. I'd be interested to know how people lived before the invention of the phonograph! What was the world like before the Beatles; before John?!"

"No, we have an extraordinary chance to find out something about the afterlife; about a proper *Russian* afterlife! And after we do, we'll go on a lecture tour across the whole of the tsardom!"

"I, for one, would like to ask whether he knows any Moscow *blatnaya* song from his era—now *that* would be a sensation! We'd sell records like hotcakes!"

"Hurry—we must commission some photos or take him to a photographer. No, wait—better if he just gave autographs. Quite the pretty kopeck, that's all I'm going to say, a very pretty kopeck, but we need to act quickly!"

Arkasha alone made no comment as he focused on devouring two sauce-doused potatoes that the great classic had left uneaten. Afterward, he had a gnawing feeling, as if he'd accidentally eaten food deliberately set on a kitchen table for the spirits of the departed; still, he *was* awfully hungry.

Konstantin Opiatovich stood up and sank a steak knife into the table with a bang!

Everyone gasped like Christ's disciples at the table of the Last Supper on hearing the betrayal soon to transpire.

Finally, Noelhard spoke up:

"Have you gone crazy?"

"That's just it! Crazy! But which one of us do you mean? Photos, The Beatles, tours! Idiots, all of you!"

Konstantin Opiatovich tapped his temple. Silence settled over the room again. Grigori Cuffovich pried the classic's dish from Arkasha's hands as the happy-go-lucky musician mopped up the last traces of sauce with a crust of bread, and took it to Katerina. For some reason, he held the plate aloft, over his head, as he passed the toilet door, taking a long and cautious step over the shroud. He whispered something to the woman as he handed over the dish. The clean coffee mug Katerina was holding fell and clattered across the floor, but did not break. Konstantin Opiatovich lifted a finger.

"He is like a rare fish, but do we have an aquarium?"

A look of horror crossed Katerina's face:

"My God! The floor's dirty, unwashed. Oh, Lordy!"

Carrying a washtub, the woman walked to the toilet door and fell to her knees as if she meant to start scrubbing the narrow passage immediately. The door slowly creaked open and Gogol stepped out of the empty tomb. It would have been a powerful moment had it not been for the foul, utterly earthy stench and Gogol tripping over the dangling cloth, causing him to plunge his right foot into Katerina's washtub with a splash. The woman squealed! With the utmost tenderness (but still breaking a long neon-painted fingernail), she immediately began washing the formerly deceased man's puckered, blackened foot. Since she had no towel, she dried the revered limb with her dyed purple locks. When Gogol retracted his leg, the woman gingerly lifted his other foot into the basin and repeated her motions. Not even Arkasha dared to stir. It was so quiet that one could have heard a pin drop or a sewing machine pant.

Gogol observed the woman absently, as if unable to understand what was happening. Then, he lifted her chin.

"It is not the impurity of the world that should

concern you, unfortunate woman, nor the impurity of your fellow man," he spoke softly, "but always and solely the impurity of your own soul."

At that moment, everyone but Vasya Kolyugin rushed to the stairs and helped the unprecedented prophet return to the table. The aid was necessary, as Gogol was breathing heavily, and it was uncertain whether he could have made it back across the slippery floorboards independently and without grasping for a banister or an invisible drainpipe.

Everyone puffed in relief while Arkasha launched into his foolish warbling once again: "Mister Gogol, might one say that you've been subject to a great misunderstanding? I recently watched an interesting documentary about you and your grave on a Russian channel. When the Chekists dug it open, they found you headless! You'd apparently suffered from malaria, but the doctors didn't realize it and your body temperature kept on falling, so you only appeared dead. Luckily, the section of your will and testament with an explicit requirement for the coffin to be ventilated with copper pipes was fulfilled. Your body temperature dropped and you apparently mummified, seeming simply to fall asleep. But your stomach stayed soft! And, as you're all too well aware now, I apologize—it left you with diarrhea!"

Gogol chuckled, wincing, and began shaping a scrap of bread (which still held some of the sauce Arkasha had scooped up) into a tiny ball.

The classic had obviously been taken aback by the

unfamiliar woman's behavior. He extended the pellet of bread to Katerina with trembling hand. The woman sank to her knees, closed her eyes, and placed the compacted sphere on her tongue like a communion wafer. A simple Estonian woman, she had no idea whether to swallow it or hold it there like a holy relic.

Leaning heavily on Katerina's shoulder, Gogol hauled himself back to his feet, a swaying monument.

"Now, take heed, you infernal, fatty mummies," Gogol slowly and hollowly croaked as if about to embark on a long speech. Yet, gripping his aching stomach with one hand, he motioned to Katerina to assist him back to the toilet. Just before the door to the golden tomb swung shut, he released a resonant and powerful fart. Like a cue striking a billiard ball or a nighttime fever engulfing an ailing man, Grigori Cuffovich Cuff succumbed at that very moment, with wild and inexplicable force, to love for that helpless, exotic woman named Katerina, who gave everything her all.

Konstantin Opiatovich quickly rose and lodged a tall barstool behind the door to the toilet so that Gogol would be incapable of getting back out on his own.

"So," the accomplished pickpocket drawled once everything was ready, "it seems we have quite the *kasha*, quite the bowl of porridge, to work out here . . ."

Part II

The Meeting

The pickpocket Konstantin Opiatovich was annoyed by anything intellectually vague. For too many years of his life, he'd been confined to the eternal "City of the Sun"; i.e. to cells in which the lights were never extinguished. Thus, the pickpocket's worldview was clear and logical; it was analytical. You do not break into a room with opaque curtains in the windows! He never involved himself in anything with an unpredictable outcome! Opiatovich had quickly come to realize life's fundamental truth: no matter what job you perform in this sublunary world, you must act in accordance with your conscience, because each has his own law. If you do something, then do it with spirit. It is the only way to accomplish anything! In the prison world, he'd noticed that a man's word is what matters most, and occasionally, he called himself a man of his word. If you say one thing, then that is what you must do. Only a man like that is respected; is approached for advice; is

given complex thieves' affairs to resolve. The unwritten
blatnoi law stated that whoever knows what's necessary
for every element of life is wiser than any academic, who
has weak spots and dangerous gaps in his knowledge.
During moments of philosophical rest, holding a sym-
bol of freedom (a honey-flavored *pryanik*), Opiatovich
enjoyed imagining himself as a drainpipe that could
neither be bent nor broken. It's not enough to believe
something in life, no, you must always be *convinced!*
Every path must be scouted beforehand; you must never
make rushed decisions. Modesty and tact are cardinal
qualities! These principles applied not only to prisoners,
but even to the world of the prison guards. The code
adhered to by officers of the cage was identical, apart
from one great difference: whereas they received orders
from above, a thief issued his own. Thus, as the years
passed, an inmate would hone his intuition in addition
to his logic. At some point, you no longer needed family
or wealth or public respect or an opinion on politics;
the mere knowledge that you were perpetually improv-
ing sufficed. This sort of man of his word soon gained
greater respect among his fellow prisoners, because only
by his own example could he guide others towards clarity, lead a questioner closer to the truth. Sometimes,
these men of their word would congregate and resolve
a particularly tight and tangled criminal knot. Great
astonishment would sometimes arise among ordinary
prisoners after a solution was given, for the men of
their word might easily decree starkly different pun-
ishments for identical acts. In truth, it was all still fair:

the men of their word were simply capable of grasping a broader reality in their arguments than a regular mortal or inmate ever could. They would always consider the acts committed by the accused based on his background, acknowledging that some had a choice but erred regardless, while others had no choice and were forced into making a mistake. This cold, pure logic occasionally swelled to such dimensions that they would even punish one of their own, one of the bigwigs seated at the table, one of the men of their word, because they, *all* those criminal gods of light, were wholly equal. There was no Zeus there, for all were Zeuses. Usually, the case involved carousal, wealth, or failure to meet one's responsibilities, and the punishment was referred to by an unusual term: "braking". Indeed, Opiatovich had also spotted men of their word among those guards who looked sympathetically on the inmates as they closed the cell door—men they knew were imprisoned for no reason; were locked up due to the undying dark affairs of injustice that arose as a consequence of family, regime, or politics. This type of guard was respected in a manner quite similar to the man of his word.

Opiatovich had made a grave mistake by meddling with the stranger and sensed it no sooner than he had stepped over the heap of sand in the tram. There'd been a curtain shrouding the gold-framed window, so to say, but he'd climbed in, regardless! You mustn't stick your nose into things you know nothing about! Later, once Opiatovich had realized with whom he was dealing, a feverish schoolboy excitement seemed to come over him—he wanted to help, to assist . . . Yet, sentimentality always came at a price! It seemed to increase with age, since one morning, he was engulfed by an inexplicable desire to write children's fairytales! He, who was a living, multivolume crime novel . . . and then, out of nowhere, fairytales! And now, he was all bogged down in this kasha!

The situation felt unusual to Opiatovich for several very logical reasons. Firstly, he would have to know Gogol's biography in order to untangle the mess. He knew it as well as anyone who had ever attended school and learned about the classics, of course, and the knowledge was still fresh in his mind, but he couldn't get at the core of his thoughts to start unwinding them like little Ariadne her ball of thread. There was no crime, no mistake! Whenever a cellmate pilfered something, he'd place it on one side of the mental scales and the *brodyak's* whole life on the other, before gradually adding inculpatory and vindicatory weights until the truth finally came to rest on the tabletop. Yet . . . no one could be blamed for Gogol having risen from the dead! For having seized the scales and flung them in the air! Never before had he encountered such a case in practice! He needed to take some time off and give gentle consideration to how to tackle this bowl of kasha.

"So," the experienced pickpocket drawled once everything was ready and Gogol had been locked in the toilet, "it seems we have quite the bowl of kasha to work on here . . ."

Opiatovich tried to speak mildly, but the echo

distorting his voice summoned memories of someone demandingly, impatiently, clanging frost-covered prison bars with a sharpened spoon. The man of his word had awoken within, but never before had the pickpocket felt such an ache in his heart as he took on a tangled mess. Dark perception slowly, almost imperceptibly, cloaked his thoughts like a black cloud over Lake Pskovskoye at night. He despised this sentimental twilight, but intuitively recognized that it was a sign of the case's exceptional complexity. It was a shame he couldn't convene a table of men of their word here in Estonia! All his former ties had been severed. The old-school men of their word in cheap gray suits would have had tea together—there was no kasha in the world that the legendary Vasya Diamond, for one, was unable to solve. Yes—Vasya! He, in particular! The man always had an old briefcase containing classic literary works handy in his cell—no doubt he'd read Gogol's complete works during his nearly fifty years in the slammer! That authority of authorities, who never introduced himself upon entering a room, but simply greeted everyone present and conversed politely until finally, and only after a whisper from a guard, you learned the identity of the man who'd arrived and quietly sat down with you for tea! He was a modest old thickly-bespectacled gentleman whose level of refinement, speed of logical thought, and adherence to the law of thieves had produced such legends that, oho-ho . . . "Yet," Opiatovich reasoned, "*I* stand here now!" Vasya Diamond had been killed by the authorities years ago at the White Swan, the final place of internment for those on death row. "I, Konstantin Opiatovich, am alive, eating a honey-flavored *pryanik* here in a Baltic province, and now I must speak for myself! Yes, I—a man of his word—will speak, too!"

"Hear me and take heed, kings of the *chanson*," declared Opiatovich, placing, out of old habit, his thumbs at a right angle on the edge of the table—the secret sign of a trial speech made by men of their word. "Something unprecedented has transpired. A great author—an intellectual giant who is studied, read, and respected by all—has risen from the dead and, like Lazarus, has trampled down death by death. This is a fact, an inarguable truth, because he is currently imprisoned—no, let us say, *confined*—in the *kamorka*. However, what has occurred must be kept a secret, for mankind and the world are not yet prepared for it. We must weigh up this whole damned kasha to find out why it has taken place, for everything in the past once possessed a deeper meaning—unlike today."

Opiatovich desperately sought words comprehensible to ordinary men occupying an emotion-filled world of twilight. In jail, he would have spoken in an entirely different manner—much more bluntly.

"Here's how we will act: henceforth, Katerina will serve him the daily special through the window until we arrive at some decision. He's got the *parasha* in there for doing his business, as well as a shelf of newer Estonian literature, just as the law requires—books that within the territory of the Russian Tsardom may only be consumed, though never read, in the toilet. He'll be able answer the call of nature and engage in culture. He'll be fed. All that remains to do is to appoint the guards—no, let us say the night watchmen. One of us must always be present because, let me stress, he might not be a prisoner at all. Anything could happen and better we be here in person. As for what to do with him—that decision we'll make over the course of the next week or so. I do not approve of informing the authorities; they'll just take him away. Just think—we have Gogol here! Gogol! Well, it's a good thing we're not dealing with Pushkin! In one week, we will decide."

Arkasha meanwhile tried to interrupt, but Konstantin Opiatovich made a quick strangling motion in his direction and he desisted (specifically, he'd had the idea that if Alla Pugacheva had risen from the dead, then they could have organized daytime apartment concerts and made a pretty kopeck).

"I'll take the first shift myself. I am the one who brought the little birdie into town and stuck him in his cage." Opiatovich surveyed the table, counting heads: there were six, including him, and if you added the waitress, seven, which was an ideal number. Seven stars in the sky had signified beginner's luck since time immemorial—consent granted from on high to anyone undertaking a complicated matter. But where was the waitress now? Ah, standing right here and listening—very good. Opiatovich addressed her politely and with the total, inarguable chivalry of a man of his word.

"Katerina, dear, please give me a spare key and hang

a sign on the door saying you will be closed for stock-taking over the next week. We will cover the costs. And men, not a single word! You decide among yourselves who will come in tomorrow night."

Out of old habit, Opiatovich placed his thumbs at right angles on the edge of the table again. Everyone was pensively silent. Then, Noelhard stood up and invited the others to join him at the bookstore. Opiatovich stepped outside for a minute to relieve himself behind an acacia bush, then returned to begin guarding the unusual prisoner. He already knew that he would be facing the most highly ranked mental task that could be encountered by a man of his word, the likes of which he would wish upon no one—not even his worst enemy.

Grigori Cuffovich took Katerina by the shoulders. She quaked with silent sobs at what she had just experienced; she quaked with the world's mad Charleston.

Konstantin Opiatovich's Watch

Katerina filled a thermos with coffee and left. Grigori locked the door. Opiatovich heard the musician test the lock from the outside several times and soothe the agitated woman. The pickpocket shined his shoes with his scrap of velvet, placed his hands on his knees, and sat up straight-backed. He needed to start thinking, pondering, considering. Since there were no windows in the space apart from one small, barred ventilation opening, the room felt extremely cozy and familiar. He enjoyed that the Novel was the kind of locale where there was no great ceremony in regard to decorations. A couple tiny orbs of light swam in the dark aquarium of the space, casting an odd frog-pond flicker over the bar countertop that resembled pallid moonlight. The illumination seeped through the silly velvet fringes of a designer-chic souvenir lamp known as an "Old Viljandi," made from three bulbs and a samovar. Hanging above the dust-coughing piano, which was perpetually out of tune and which Grigori Cuffovich sneeringly referred to as the "manure crate," was a large painting of local Viljandi cultural celebrities. The wretched picture had been made by the sentimental old drunkard who had taught Petrusha everything he knew and had a studio behind the railway station. Unfortunately, the idea (which had sounded like a stroke of genius at first) of creating a work of art that would depict the small town's important persons and subsequently selling it to the city government had not worked out. Simply put, no one could recognize themselves (even the women's heads resembled tiny potatoes that were impossible to tell apart), and had the names not been listed in old-fashioned cursive at the bottom edge of the canvas, then correctly identifying anyone would have been a hopeless endeavor. The city government's discerning Estonian janitor—a former pharmacist named Lavrenty Yuryevich Pribolotny, who had drunk himself to the bottom of the bottle and was nicknamed "Swamp Monster" by his former colleagues—shooed the money-grubbing excuse for a painter out of the building the moment he glimpsed the utterly failed physiognomies. His sort didn't even hang around the seedy Kantreküla Pharmacy distribution point when free drugs were handed out on Christmas Eve! Reeling from the fiasco, the artist ultimately stumbled into the Novel with the painting in tow, where he asked Katerina whether an old-school work of art might, perhaps, fit in nicely above the piano (the old man respectfully referred to the upright as the "Black Swan"). Katerina showed him pity and acquiesced, but only on condition that the old man hang it himself and unscrew the light bulbs on either side. The old man gratefully accepted the proposal, and when handed a shot of Kiiu Bashnya, he even called Katerina a brilliant little quail! The clock on the wall had stopped. Giving its pendulum a push had yielded no results for a long time already. The whole mechanism would need to be disassembled and removed from the clock box for thorough inspection. However, Opiatovich did not rise from his chair—he didn't want to make a single superfluous movement today. Bizarrely, an old memory was doggedly replaying in his head, like an invisible hand flattening a diapositive over an illuminated bulb.

He appeared to be at the small café across from the enormous Hotel Moscow in that very city. To his right was a merry company of cultural folk, apparently artists, who were drinking and carousing. They were clamoring about some great art commission, a competition to design vodka labels. In his notebook, a thin man wearing an orange dress shirt and an exceedingly *prostoye* cotton coat was sketching the monumental structure across the street: the huge, recently opened, prominent, state hotel. Opiatovich could tell it was an incredibly skillful drawing. Simultaneously and almost just as masterfully, Opiatovich lifted a yellow leather wallet from the man's pocket, even though it deeply pained him to do so. One master does not steal from another! Yet, the memory was suddenly dispelled, as someone was shaking him. He had drunk himself to a stupor and somehow ended up in a room at that same prominent hotel. It was night, but the floor manager had opened

Opiatovich's door and she was now rousing the man
to tell him he must leave at once and move to another
hotel, because a state funeral was to be held there in
the morning. Cold air from outside struck Opiatovich's
face, as the forceful middle-aged woman threw open
the window. The Kremlin flickered between the curtains. He had to leave at once because the place had to
be vacated by morning; he had to get up. Opiatovich
was shaken—he was young, lanky, hung over, and had
violated the laws of thieves.

Opiatovich opened his eyes and froze. On the table
in front of him at the Novel was an open bottle of
Stolichnaya Russian Vodka bearing its famous logo: a
drawing of the Hotel Moscow! And next to the half-li-
ter bottle was a tea glass tied with a black mourning
ribbon! Then, out of the darkness, someone lisping
through a gap in his teeth began whistling his favorite song, "Murka"! To top it all, it was, as Opiatovich
immediately realized, an earlier version, not his beloved
blatnaya tune! The legendary melody sounded much
more ancient and gravellier . . . the age-old Estonian
Viljandi Jail arrangement! Some of the words had been
replaced—the Chekist Murka was killed by Estonian
Forest Brothers, as a result of which there were slight
hiccups in the rhythm. Opiatovich listened, sucking
in the horror of that whole moment. Never in his life
had he heard or seen anything more absurd or illogical!
With all his might, he kicked away the café table and
everything on it, and in a couple of inhuman bounds
he had ascended to the balcony. The toilet door was

open—the space was empty! Sinister Estonian moonlight poured onto his face through the small, open window. His surroundings were suddenly hostile to their very core! Opiatovich didn't look back. Only when he paused beneath a streetlight in front of the children's music school did his right elbow start to ache, as it appeared he'd sustained an injury. Opiatovich took a couple of deep breaths—his shirt was soaked, and he'd left his hat behind. His throbbing, swelling arm was the only logical object amid the icy terror and illogical Estonian fog rising from the lake below. He quickly made his way home; the familiar surroundings suddenly appeared frightening, altered. The pickpocket felt as if the shadows of lost souls were standing silently in their hundreds on either side of his escape route, like bayonets guarding a convoy; the rustling of the bushes in human tongue made the streetlights sway. Passing the officers' club, it even seemed for a moment like one of the large wooden pillars was on the verge of crashing down on him with a groan from its place beneath the pediment. Opiatovich glanced fearfully over his shoulder—the wooden triangle and pillars remained firmly in place, but standing in the middle of the road, far in the distance, somewhere back near the Novel, was a tall, dark figure. Its right arm was raised high and bent at an inhuman angle.

Opiatovich fled home. For several hours, he sat at the kitchen table and tried to figure out why he had been punished with such a vivid, cruel vision. Sometime after midnight, he began to grasp a certain monumental logic to what had transpired. An extremely powerful force or highly-polished system had "milked" him that night, so to say; had made him its cow. The sole moment of weakness in Opiatovich's life's story had been found and flung before him—the only story he could remember in that cheap electric paradise; an incident that took place in his younger days, at the Hotel Moscow, in which he had violated thieves' law several-fold. Today, a master much greater than he had demonstrated his might and ultimate knowledge, playing a more brilliantly polished fortepiano, and, as the true Zeus, had loosed an arrow straight into the long-extinguished darkness of his memories; he had urinated, godlike, straight through a filter onto his fundamental philosophy, drenching his entire subconscious in that evil rain and causing it now to stink like an unbearable *parasha*.

The pickpocket slept no more that night. He fished a slim velvet mourning ribbon out of a Yalta jewelry box adorned with tiny seashells, and fastened it to his coat lapel. He was guilty, but even so, he was prepared to enter the endgame with as much dignity as he could muster. The entire world, and especially Viljandi, suddenly appeared utterly hostile. It felt like every building in that town, which had been constructed with logic, precision, and order, had risen against Opiatovich and was now accusing him, a man of his word, of murky dealings! Every angle, arch, and row of bricks whispered indecipherable Estonian-language spells and theorems of the utmost infrangible logic in regard to how and by whom all had been created in that place. With each passing moment, he could sense the terrifying convoy of invisible bayonets that were growing sharper and sharper, marching closer and closer, just like on the night of the Estonian deportations not so long ago, just a few years past, which Opiatovich had witnessed by chance. The pickpocket steered clear of politics, but he still recalled as a vision of utmost horror the scene that unfolded near a forever-closed metro station a few days later. The screaming. The pandemonium. The endless dusk and sadness.

He finally fell asleep with his clothes on and, having slept through the entire day, awoke only as a new evening fell. Opiatovich grabbed a couple dried breadcrusts from the windowsill, popped them into his mouth, and went outside, hurrying in the direction of the bookstore. It was very cold outside. The other men had drawn lots and the lowest card in Noelhard's deck had gone to Vasya, who was to spend the next night in the Novel. Opiatovich wordlessly handed him the key and then, out of habit, slunk towards the tram stop. Once aboard, he rested his head against the chilly evening windowpane and fell asleep at his post, there in the rocking vehicle, for the very first time in his life.

Vasya Kolyugin's Watch

Everything at the used bookstore named Bookstore appeared the same at first glance. As an exception to the rule, however, Noelhard had allowed his friends to spend the night inside. Badenov and Arkasha were still sound asleep in the back room, the latter enjoying a genuinely hippie dream about strolling around a tiny Eastern city named Mukina, his baggy pants heavily laden with gold. Luckily, he was wearing a small coat in the dream, so the barbaric passersby noticed nothing strange. Nevertheless, circumstances were far from the ordinary, as two suns shone in the sky, scrutinizing him so closely that at intervals, in order to cover his tracks, he had to take cover, adopting the fetal position in nonexistent empty rooms. When he did so, the brighter of the two suns would often swoop in close to the window, its giant eye boring into the room and the feigning sleeper.

Vasya had no objections to spending the night at the Novel in the company of the bar's fantastic sound equipment. He turned left onto Post Street from the red-brick Hotel London, walked past the Day Center for the Disabled (which he both feared and despised), then headed straight for the nighttime locale. He stopped for a quick smoke in the park next to the old classical court-house, poking through a trashcan to see what brands of cologne people were drinking these days. Vasya regarded drunkards with sympathy and compassion, because just like them, he rejected all significant ideologies. He'd been on a path to nowhere ever since his younger days and believed that now he was getting pretty close. Vasya's whole life had taken a turn for the better and the more colorful after ending up on his Beatles kick. If only there were more—if only more of these short days were granted to him to build a Beatles temple dedicated to love and music!

Even from several yards away, he could tell that the door to the Novel was closed; a sign that read CLOSED FOR STOCKTAKING hung there, illuminated by the powerful floodlight on the battlemented parapet of the music school. The neglected, unoccupied clubhouse above the bar was on the verge of collapsing; just *yeli-yeli* still erect. No plans had been made for old wooden buildings of its kind since the Estonians had gone. Actually, all it took was for the drainpipes to be stolen, and the whole damp-walled wooden palace would reek of dry rot and rapid disintegration, like an old woman who yearns to embark on her eternal journey as swiftly as possible after her husband dies.

The door was locked and wet to the touch, but a

narrow shaft of light showed that the pickpocket
Opiatovich—a man who always dotted his i's and
crossed his t's—had sensibly left the lights on inside.
The only possible explanation for the unexpected draft
that billowed out as he opened the door was that the
backdoor from kitchen to the courtyard had been left
open. "I bet the thief went out for a smoke," Vasya
reckoned as he eyed the gigantic painting of local cultural figures that hung right across from the door. How
ideally Lennon's image would fit in with the rest! How
pitiful those small-town poetry prima donnas, newspaper lackeys, and caricaturists all were. And, what's
more, how miserably they'd been portrayed! Fans of
The Beatles would have made such a fine club in the
space! Oh, how the kaleidoscope-eyed girls would have
shaken and danced around the room! But . . . *nathing is
reel! Strawberry feelds farever!* The Novel's daily specials
were still quite alright.

Oddly, Opiatovich had even left a candle lit on the
piano! Vasya wasn't very concerned, though—thieves
were relatively sentimental people. Whenever he went
down to the lake in summer and listened to a-hard-
day's-night stuff out of his cassette-box, the beach was
usually packed with tattooed citizens. In nice weather,
the onion domes and Madonnas tattooed on veiny
backs created such a crucifix-led procession of *ay-fiil-
fayne* . . . people played cards, drank vodka, and—just
to pass the time—might beat the hell out of a motorcy-
clist who flat out refused to pay a nonexistent parking

ticket to a provoked and wobbling authority! No doubt
Opiatovich had played the piano (what else?), maybe
singing a little tune about an evening church bell or a
reddening viburnum bush, or else had been whistling
that accursed "Murka" of his! Vasya shuffled up the
stairs, placed his ear against the toilet door to listen for
Gogol, and then went to pull the heavy iron courtyard
door shut with a bang. He grabbed a beer from the
refrigerator and stuck a cassette into the music machine
behind the counter. However, his first long-awaited sip
of musical feel-alright-*khorosho* melted away instantaneously. Sitting on the sofa down in the bar area was an
unfamiliar old gentleman in a vest and suit coat, glaring
at him intensely!

Since the individual bore a striking resemblance to a
cartoon character, Vasya tried simply shaking his head
and opening his eyes again . . . However, the little old
man, who had a rare and old-fashioned watch chain
carved out of a single piece of wood draped across his
chest, was still staring him right in the eye!

"*Gad pless yew!*" Vasya croaked to the stranger with
a feeble wave of his beer can. What in the blazes! It was
clear that whoever he was (probably Katerina's father-in-
law or someone of the sort), everything was screwed! He
could go ahead and forget about having his nice evening
chill! But still . . . so what? Maybe it was someone will-
ing to discuss the temple or listen to *she-lavs-yew* stuff?
A person's a person, even though, based on the man's
appearance, he wasn't exactly a flower child . . .

Vasya was about to fetch another beer from the refrigerator, but the gentleman suddenly materialized behind him, introducing himself and ushering him to the table. He claimed his name was "Fon Glayn Éclair" or something to the effect.

"Yes, I am a teetotaler, and I recommend it to you, too, if you are involved in temple construction," said the elderly magical-mystery-tour man. The stranger's hands were covered in intricate old Baltic German high-*blat-nyak* tattoos—female German names with spiraling vignettes. Etched into his neck was a crooked coat of arms that included a mighty purple crocodile smoking a cigar. He amiably slid his arm under the dazed Vasya's to prop him up. The putative Fon Glayn's suit was far too immaculate . . .

"I do presume it will not escape from there?" the watch-chain man conspiratorially asked Vasya as they passed the toilet door. Ah, so the stranger knew about Gogol!

Confound it all! Vasya shook his head. Lying on the table was a giant leather-bound photo album titled *Album*. It didn't appear to be the Novel guestbook—the names of the bar's more esteemed clients were simply scrawled on the wall behind the counter. The old man had apparently brought the hefty tome with him.

They sat down. Vasya's beer tasted like water or stale pumpkin juice, which is to say he didn't enjoy it at all. The creases in the old man's pants were as sharp as the alpine passes where fascists were said to have pursued the ancient-sound-of-music Beatles family. The atmosphere was menacing. Nevertheless, Vasya could tell the gentleman was likely wealthy and foreign, and what's more, he was already aware of the plan to build the temple, probably having heard of it from Katerina.

"The idea—we really do have this idea—is to erect a temple of love in honor of Lennon, so to say!" As he spoke, Vasya produced a ceramic pocket model of the temple from his coat pocket and set it on the leather-bound book.

"Is that so!" exclaimed the fool-on-the-hill old man, displaying what appeared to be genuine interest. "And where is this wonderful castle to arise?"

Now, Vasya rubbed his hands together and launched into his usual well-rounded overview of the whole plan: nine stories, height 270 feet, submarine elevator, *vechnoi* bliss, etc., etc. Just in case his listener turned out to be a rich old Helsinki-businessman-patron-guy along the lines of the millionaire Osmo Vanska, Vasya threw in a pure crystal Lennon statue with three live bear cubs playing inside, in order to forge something of a connection to regular people. The old man nodded and listened attentively, the cigar-smoking crocodile on his neck settling deeper into its chair and puffing arrogant clouds of smoke.

Vasya lifted the temple model into the air by way of conclusion, because that very moment, the idea came to him that once a year, on the anniversary of Lennon's death, giant helicopter blades would elevate the entire holy structure above the profane earth, even if only for an instant! Lennon's statue would be like a symbolic lighthouse, and the bears would all stare in the right direction, of course. They would need to have a full-time trainer with them at all times, anyway, as well as an attractive cleaning woman holding a handsome bucket.

"I must congratulate you, young man," said the old man. "You have everything nicely planned out. I once had a palm house like that next to my castle."

This Fon-Glayn-something opened the album and showed Vasya two little ponds complete with fountains and bear statues that had once been situated in an out-building. Vasya's heart leapt to the rafters with joy! For the first time ever, someone was taking him truly, truly seriously! And not just someone, but a citizen-castel-lan-*knyaz*! What point was there in discussing such a grand structure with the kopeck-pinching Noelhard or Arkasha, who slept on mats in hallways? Here was someone who himself had built a castle, a palm house—even a hulking crocodile and, if Vasya understood him correctly, a towering statue of his son! Take, for example, the idea of putting in large display windows! He'd never have come up with something like that on his own! Natural, unpolished, locally-sourced stones joined together with cement; shapes that appeared to grow right up out of the ground! The invaluable stranger also spoke at length about offices—how the working environment of the director of a future company like that would have to look. He recommended putting up framed educational aphorisms and kindly wrote one for Vasya:

If you ever stick your digits
In a stranger's pack
Soon, all your dearest riches
Will be carried off by rats!

For a wall of the red-plush bedroom behind the office, however, the stranger-Tsarskoye-Selo-Fabergé-meringue recommended a jollier verse:

Oh, we'd packed our bellies tight
With all those sugary sweets
And Boo and Baby'd stretch out for the night
After mounds of scrumptious eats

Just like that age-old Esel
We find ourselves slothful now
And that missus tante Tharese
Is to blame for being like sows!

Vasya had sunk deep into thought and noticed two bizarre things. Whenever the old-man-Khottabych-gold-coin spoke about something, the photo album opened to the given page all on its own. Secondly, when Fon-Glayn pronounced the word "album", he did so somehow Arabically—somehow peculiarly, like "*Al-Bumm*"—and with a rustling of pages, the right pictures would appear. It was amazing, of course, but still frightful! Thirdly, the old man kept returning to an odd un-Beatles-like theory about how a temple builder must sleep only three hours a day, must not consume alcohol, and must practice vegetarianism. Otherwise, he said, the castle, palm house, and statues would never be finished—you'd simply lack the strength required to erect a hallucinatory room of transformation. This glorification of work sounded distinctly back-in-the-USSR! Why all the plush if you can't drink a beer and listen to *tikket-to-rayde*? Vasya was especially annoyed by the stranger's assertions that the greatest construction work was only just beginning. Specifically, Fon Balticgemanovich droned on about how he'd delivered milk with a goat, built cellars, and surveyed properties in the middle of the woods for a residential development somewhere around the Nömme and Olde-Mustamäe districts where there was now a large Estonian cemetery. But what was the point to the whole song and dance if bliss wasn't what mattered most! If you couldn't lie at Lennon's feet, in a manner of speaking, and simply listen to *all-yew-need-iz-laav*? No, there was no need for a temple like that! If people constantly need you to attend to things after it's ready, then there's no need for a temple at all! Vasya felt his life's goal had been sent spinning! There, on the stage of rainbow-striped horizons of expectation, a hand covered in German-language tattoos was closing the curtains of reason on the prima donna Pointless, who till this very moment had always sung to Vasya with spectacular beauty, genuineness, and Beatles-ness! Yuck!

Suddenly, the clock struck midnight. When Vasya lifted his swimming gaze from the *Al-Bumm*, his head pounding, he saw the whole floor of the Novel was covered in cassette tape, which was being spewed at a rising tempo from the hissing slot of the cassette player. Vasya leapt to his feet. The old man had vanished! The toilet door, behind which Gogol was confined, was being pummeled by wild blows from within! If it weren't for the fine wooden watch chain that ran across the cheap door as if it were a peasant's hairy chest, then the evilest of all forces would be let loose instantaneously! The door was being charged with inhuman strength! "Away from here!" Vasya thought. Moments later, he was back outside in the park; in the blinding beam of the floodlight that glared down from the children's music school. A gut-wrenching roar came from the bar and, like the squealing of a goat, an old women's bicycle chained to the handrail began slowly, unnaturally to buckle. Vasya ran home, never once looking back at the Novel, or probably his entire life up to that point.

Love *is* the only thing that sets us apart from animals—beasts do not listen to The Beatles; they have no tapes nor cassette players. What paranormal force could raise a hand against a recording of sacred music or a cassette of The Beatles? Swaying from side to side in helplessness, Vasya sat in his cramped room—suddenly, he no longer felt any interest in the temple. The ghost was right: in the end, he'd have been hitched to that silly cultural center like a zoo director. How terrible it was that it hadn't crossed his mind earlier! Anti-bliss!

Vasya took a syringe filled with *shniakok* (an ambiguous narcotic substance) out from under one half of a soccer ball, where it had lain, untouched, for many years. For the first time in his life, he had no desire to listen to music. It was as if a candle had been snuffed out—he spun off the wheel of *saṃsāra* into the muddy *moksha* of Everyman-justice, and fell asleep at the feet of a crystal Lennon.

Noelhard's Watch

All day, Noelhard had been intending to look in at the Novel after closing the bookstore, to check if everything was fine. Vasya *was* a renowned airhead, what with all his ob-la-di ob-la-da! Furthermore, Gogol should probably be let out for a walk or a smoke. While he did so, Noelhard could perhaps prod him for authoritative knowledge on the occult and the afterlife. In any event, he felt he had to visit the locale that evening; his heart was simply not at peace.

Noelhard parked his van in front of the Novel. An old, buckled, woman's bicycle was hanging from the handrail next to the stairs! Oh, those blasted Dushanbe hippies! Those Stalinabad Beatles!

It was as he feared: the door was ajar. Sensual and rather pleasant music was drifting out through the long fringe curtains. Standing in the center of the room was the museum watchwoman Zinaida Prokofyevna! Vasya was nowhere to be seen . . .

Noelhard slapped his hands against his pantlegs, greeted the old maid, and asked, emphasizing every word:

"Vasya. Went. Out. Hmm?"

Zinaida Prokofyevna seemed momentarily confused by the unexpected inquiry, moistening her lips with a stunningly beautiful tongue and gesturing towards the sofa. Today, for some inexplicable reason, Noelhard saw a woman more youthful and vigorous than the hag he'd often encountered at the market. Even the bosom beneath the snow-white Russian blouse she wore was somehow very . . . very . . . energetic!

"Isn't Vasya here?"

"Vasya went home. He felt unwell, poor little thing—listened to too much music!"

Just then, Noelhard noticed the entire floor was indeed covered in ribbonlike, ruined, "crocodile-chewed" cassette tape. What kind of a Beatles orgy had he thrown here?! Oh, Vasya, Vasya . . .

"Katerina asked me to clean up. She's already fed Gogol and taken him for his walk today. He wasn't all that fond of the walk, but he did have a good appetite. Apparently, he was very tired and wished to get back to the toilet as soon as he could."

Noelhard was caught off balance. Women really were utterly contradictory beings—did they think Gogol was some kind of a poodle? That all he did was eat, sleep, and walk? "That Vasya and I need to have a little talk," Noelhard thought, making a mental note and, in spite of himself, taking a seat on the bar's squat *divanchik*.

Zinaida sat down on a chair and hung one leg over her other knee like a chubby church chandelier.

"That Mister Gogol of yours had some very intriguing things to say, don't you know!"

"He did?"

"He said he's quite accustomed to having conversation at the lunch table. He was rather delighted to see Katerina made him pancakes, *pampushky*, and *kut'ya*. He said those were his favorite childhood foods."

"I'll make a note of the honorable Gogol's preferred menu," said Noelhard, and pretended to pencil something into his notebook, although quite licentiously, he was actually ogling the woman's large knees—they were as white as a *reshetilov's* sheepskin! Zinaida's *zapaska* was extremely high, allowing glimpses of her underpants. *Oy blyad'*! Noelhard's whole body was heating up!

"Katerina recorded everything he said; it was just like attending a lecture. After trying some of Katerina's *vareniki*, Mister Gogol spoke about love at great length!"

"Is that so? You don't still happen to have what Katerina wrote, do you?"

The scrap of paper was dreadfully smeared, but her old-fashioned handwriting was clearly legible. Was Katerina really so well-educated? Had she attended the Viljandi School for Girls back in Estonian times, perhaps?

Noelhard couldn't believe his eyes as he scanned the page. It was titled "The Magnetic Theory of Love"— precisely what fascinated him most in the world, and on which topic so few books and documents had been

written! It began with Ficino's belief that love's heat
fills the blood, and thence veered eastward, bringing
in the concept of Qigong—the Chinese equivalent
of immaterial fluid! Gogol had made a brief but riv-
eting detour into the paraphysiology of ancient cultures and echoed Plato himself, who linked love and
fever. Noelhard hadn't enjoyed anything this much in
ages. And it was merely the introduction to his theory!
Oh, oh, oh! Could it be true? Could Gogol honestly be
quoting M. Fool's lost masterpiece *The Passion for You*?
Yes, and it seemed he even addressed the so-called Milan
volume, which was lost in the nineteenth century and
was said to propose a mysterious theory of three types
of love—specifically claiming that there exists platonic,
physical-emotional, and magnetic *lyubov*'! And that the
latter is, in fact, the deepest bedrock of any kind of
love. Noelhard's hands began to tremble as he read further, for Gogol had outlined to the women the entire
magnetic structure of the Eros, introducing the mag-
ical/magnetic apology of love and implementing the
concept of schizophrenia; i.e. the standpoint that in a
true romantic situation, one's thoughts become those of
the other. Noelhard shuddered with enthusiasm. Gogol
was just getting to what mattered most—to the core of
gender magic; to the eternal conjunction of binary fantasies, which pulverized all temporal ties with its metaphysical force; which erased history and induced a permanent shift of consciousness, delivering exaltation and
immortality; delivering the truth of existence! Here and
there, he could already pick out the word "shungite"!

He had been right all along! It was shungite that should bring about the ultimate catalyst! Ooh! Ooh! Before launching himself upon the final words, Noelhard lifted his gaze in prayer and was suddenly struck breathless . . . Zinaida was sitting across from him as naked as snow. The goddess's breasts were dancing the *hopak* such that Noelhard could no longer tell the difference between kliros and clitoris! A church choir sang from the apex of the shungite pyramid and at last, Zinaida allowed her *namitka*—her wimple; her headdress—to fall behind her. As Noelhard collapsed, groaning, into the woman's embrace, he noticed over her shoulder that the door to the Novel was wide open, and the cell was empty. At that moment, the woman bit into Noelhard as if he were a little ball of bread, then choked him to unconsciousness with unanticipated masculine force.

Bully J. Badenov and Arkady Dmitrievich Severny's Watch

When Badenov and Arkasha awoke, the bookstore named Bookstore was empty. Neither Opiatovich the pickpocket, Noelhard the shungite king, nor Vasya the Beatles hippie were there. Cuffovich the guitarist had been generally absent lately, because rumor had it that he was consumed with infatuation for Katerina. The bookstore's door stood wide open and cold air gushed in. Wind flapped the pages of the cheapest and least interesting books, which were stacked between the inner and outer doors.

"Oh, what a *yerundisha*, what a *depresnyak* this is!" Arkasha moaned, elbowing the sleeping Badenov. "The door's open—go close it!"

Badenov winced drowsily.

"You need to close the door; otherwise, Mr. Squall will come in," Arkasha droned, staring at the ceiling.

Badenov was on his feet at once. Mr. Squall was a

stumpy Estonian who'd gone raving mad during the property-ownership reforms carried out by the tsardom. It was said that he lived in the abandoned puppet theater across the street and was armed. Indeed, he behaved like a puppet or a introverted little child, climbing onto chairs wherever he gained entry and searching for a cake into which he could jump. He always carried around a small cracked pocket mirror, which he used to reflect his surroundings and into which he insisted everyone look. Regardless, Noelhard would occasionally feed him, because the man *had* formerly owned the building and the storefront that now housed the used bookstore. Mr. Squall had been spared deportation, for some reason—no doubt he was too childlike, even compared to children. No, the door needed to be closed. Pale-faced, Badenov sat down on a chair next to the door like a sentry.

Arkasha had lit an unfiltered cigarette and seemed to be enjoying himself—it was, in any case, one hundred times better to wake up here than in a stairwell somewhere. When your belly is full and you've had a good night's sleep, you feel like a balalaika is playing your life's rhythm! With negative emotions, on the other hand, you can even turn the snow black! Life's accordion pattern will never be ideal (something Arkasha knew all too well). He nibbled on another cookie from the pack Noelhard had left on the windowsill. You've got to glean joy from the little things, too! Certainly not from little Mr. Squall!

Bully J. was busy ruminating as well. He'd just come up with a striking comparison: culture is merely

a transparent film laid over life's horrors. As soon as
you grip a handle or a knob more tightly, something
cold-callous-bacterial is revealed. In many a sense, he
already longed for the little room upstairs where he
could listen to that transparent film or tape of culture
on a record player as he serenely reclined on the sofa.
Even so, it was a great right-blessing-honor to be in the
company of a living national talent: Arkasha, who was
almost like Presley or Vysotsky!

Once Badenov had rested a little, he took a deep
breath and peered out at the darkened street.

"We should probably get going, Arkasha. It's our
turn to be on watch today."

Arkasha lifted an eyebrow.

"Is it really tomorrow already? Are you sure?"

Arkasha thought his friend was mistaken, and in fact,
he was right. Noelhard had left for the Novel only a few
hours earlier.

Badenov brought out a large thermos of coffee.
Incense burned before the icon in the corner and a large
gold-framed mirror on the wall reflected the room in a
jumbled, dusky way, like Moscow buried in fog at twilight. Arkasha gradually began to liven up.

"You know, we should introduce Gogol to contem-
porary ghetto music! I bet you he won't like any of that
new rubbish. Men always expressed themselves very
concisely back in the day. I reckon we share the same
view on the topicality of songs: a person-artist-per-
former isn't a newspaper that should immediately report
on the poppycock going on around him, you know!"

"Still," Arkasha continued, pulling on Noelhard's bathrobe and making a sweeping gesture at the cozy little space, "since it is an extraordinary situation, we can come straight back afterward!"

Life was simmering in nighttime Viljandi. A raucous pandemonium was coming from the Armenian restaurant nearby. To Badenov's amazement, Arkasha set off toward it!

"A true Georgian always begins his evening and his women-chasing with a certain saying. I like Orientalism! The burning grassland feeds my horse and the eastern steppe embraces me, as the words to the song go!"

Bully J. was baffled by what connection the Armenian restaurant and the Georgian saying might share, but Arkasha, clutching his bathrobe tightly around him in his tiny musician's fists, was already hurrying along toward the dining establishment of dubious repute.

"Anxiety crept into my soul the moment my cigarette went out today—the sparks flew right into the fireplace, I'm telling you!" Badenov heard Arkasha say as he strode ahead, panting.

"Do we really need to go there rather than to the Novel?"

Arkasha paused for a moment. They'd come to the small Russian Orthodox church that had recently been erected in place of the dilapidated Estonian Ruby Cinema. A service was underway. As they stood there, a woman hurriedly exited the place of worship. Arkasha crossed himself and bowed low to the ground. Badenov couldn't tell whether he was bowing before the church or the woman, though it wasn't impossible that the man might simply be playing a trick and bowing to himself, instead.

"Who was that?" Badenov asked, shivering.

Arkasha stared mournfully at the woman as she receded.

"A pure soul . . . a pure soul!"

"He will never be happy, that Arkasha," Badenov thought to himself as they continued on their way. "Such talent, even though he has nothing—no wife, no car, not even a place to call home. He tortures himself, burning like a Hindu candle that longs to be snuffed out; that yearns for eternal fading-*moksha-nirvanka*. But he finds no peace . . . all grown up, but wounded in spirit."

At the Armenian establishment, eastern music was screeching over the speakers and a few men were playing a board game with dice beneath the plastic palm trees. Badenov immediately recognized Caesar, Butterball, and Murderer—three of the most unpleasant Post Street criminals. Arkasha went into the toilet, where he remained for quite a long time, and when he returned, he stared at the men with a peculiar sense of jealousy and resentment.

"E-hee-he-hee! There's a genuine, honest-to-goodness Japanese girl in the toilet—as real as can be and quite the geisha-slut-*ikebana*!" he proclaimed, sitting down, enveloped by an adrenalized aura. "Who would've thought it, huh? Total extra-class orgasm origami!"

No sooner had he uttered these words than an

unearthly woman with a blindingly white face drifted through the room in a purple dress, her miniature, almost living-doll-like steps carrying her to the shashlik patio. Her thick wooden shoes creaked on the cheap tiles.

"Ah, my goddess—what a prosecutor's daughter!" Arkasha moaned, clamping his cigarette between his teeth. It was as if Arkasha had been sliced in half in the restroom: his hands trembled as he lit a match, though his face had acquired an exceptionally calm and even determined expression. Badenov recognized that Arkasha had sunk into his most dangerous state: one in which he was indifferent to the whole world. The fast-living man ordered a large decanter of vodka; Badenov had a shot of Stary Graf Kaliningrad brandy. Arkasha had apparently gotten everything he'd ever wished for in the toilet, as he was humming a little tune about a girl named Vera who lives in a prosecutor's household and takes a wrong turn in life. The final verse of the *blatnaya* ditty spoke of an unhappy love for a thief, a convict's black bench, and the breathtaking Vera's father—a prosecutor overcome by heartache, who merely drinks and weeps. It was an upbeat song (at least in the manner Arkasha performed it), and apparently the current expression of his sick heart's hangover-like romance; like a ruby in a damp hill of ash, having fallen into a fireplace.

"Noelhard always insists that one should read books," giggled Arkasha, grabbing the decanter and pouring himself a drink.

"The way I see it is that books really are the only things that tie us to history at all," he continued, still holding the crystalware. "Even so, they can just stand there, and nothing will ever happen to them—the bookstore is full of books, right?! Vodka and women—now *those* will spoil if they're left lying around! They'll go sour and wrinkly! Even the Japanese know it! Every *kid* knows it! Therefore, let the seagull play itself—I'm going to drink booze and leer at the ladies . . . That's the type of seagull I am! Music's important, too, of course—like that song goes: I left you because I found a guitar. When there's no more vodka or women, then all you've got left is a little song."

Suddenly, standing next to their table was an old woman with Far Eastern facial contours, who was wearing a shapeless tracksuit and holding a small child that looked just like . . . Mr. Squall!

"British sailor," rasped the woman in a hideous voice, jerking Arkasha painfully by the shoulder. "Your child, remember?"

Badenov felt ill at ease; he was completely flummoxed. What was that Mr. Squall doing here? Arkasha smirked, not even glancing in the woman's direction. Instead, he refilled his glass.

"Miss, we're on different buses; on different routes in life, as they say!"

"What does she want? Do you know this old hag?" asked Badenov timorously. "What's Mr. Squall doing here?"

On hearing this, Arkasha turned and gaped directly

at the woman. He was suddenly dumbfounded, as if he'd glimpsed something intimately familiar in the gaunt Japanese face. Nauseous, he stumbled to the toilet without once looking at the child-Squall. The woman followed in hot pursuit, but by the time Badenov got up and made it to the toilet door, it was wide open and the witch was nowhere to be seen.

Arkasha was in his undershirt, trembling and leaning over the sink. An inexplicable force had molded Noelhard's bathrobe into a bizarre Japanese terrycloth stool in front of him, the two sleeves serving as stiff drainpipe chair legs. The monstrosity was whining like a small child! For a moment, Badenov could hear it as clear as day. Pervading the Armenians' otherwise painstakingly clean bathroom was an unbearable musty stench, a potpourri of intestinal upset, church incense, and nursing-home urine. Arkasha had shoved his hand into his mouth and was gagging something unintelligible as saliva dribbled from his lips. It sounded like a toxic breath escaping the pierced, shriveled lung of a Jewish rabbi crying out in Hebrew: "Gyyyyyyyhhh-gggggyyyyyl!"

Part III

In the Garden of Eden

The guitarist-ignoramus-*kvakushka*-guy Grigori Cuffovich called home from a payphone next to the bicycle shop. Lyuba listened wordlessly. She'd already figured out that her husband was involved with someone several days ago, but the call still came as a flash of lightning from clear skies. Arriving at his crumbling home, Grigori sat down on the leather couch and covered his face with his right hand. Lyuba was just on her way out to the consignment shop. She stood in the center of the room wearing her coat and boots, her reflection glittering both in profile and full face in the dozens of crystal vases displayed in the vitrines. The hand shrouding Grigori's face was nowhere reflected, only quivering and shrinking more and more, turning increasingly transparent—his cheap silver music-school ring seemed about to slip off his shriveled finger and fall to the floor with a cacophonous clatter. Lyuba had readied two suitcases, one of which had long stood in disuse on top of a cupboard and faintly reeked of cat piss. She was shaken to the core by what had happened and left without saying a word.

Grigori Cuffovich Cuff stood up and looked around the room despairingly. The carousel of his thoughts was spinning so fast that he couldn't pick out a single object to take with him. As a little boy, he'd stood before the ticket booth of a Czech funfair, unable to choose between the frightening and the less-unnerving attractions. Ultimately, almost intentionally, he grabbed the silliest and least useful of his possessions: from the wall, two bayonets (one Swiss-made, the other Norwegian) that hung between bear paintings; and from the umbrella basket, a metal-handled walking cane that imitated a gnarled stick. From the icon corner, he slipped into his pocket a watch that was ticking away on a gaudy metal tray, as well as a gold brooch with a blue gem that he'd worn on the front of his *ushanka* when ice skating in his youth. Then, suddenly, achingly, like sticking one's tongue to a playground carousel in the freezing cold, he came to his senses and started tossing underwear, socks, and a couple of bow ties into a suitcase. His guitar and cables were always packed and ready next to the door to be taken out for a walk. Approaching their tiny icon corner, he crossed himself from left to right, took one last look around the apartment where he'd spent the happiest days of his life, and left, dragging the bulky suitcases painfully thumping down the stairs behind him, like all his unborn children.

An unexpected snow had fallen. Grigori stood

uneasily in front of the building—his suitcases had stuck fast in a drift, his guitar had bounced back painfully against his hip. The old woman who lived on the third floor and was always squabbling with the other residents hadn't picked up the snow shovel, her reasoning being that if she trimmed a mysterious shrub somewhere behind the building—one known only to her—then she had the right to refuse any other chores. The old crone had also scrawled this (with several spelling mistakes) in the bottom margin of the cleaning schedule, and as a result, on her cleaning days, the white substance accumulated more and more outside the front door. Grigori Cuffovich's anger at the old crone rose one last time, but to his own surprise, he swiftly and sentimentally forgave her, instead worrying about what life here would be like without him.

A blue taxi with shabby upholstery delivered him all too quickly to Katerina's building. He heaved his suitcases into the entryway and decided to use the bathroom before leaving his new home. The toilet was cozy and snug, but particularly provocative was the fact that it was in no way soundproof. Caged birds twittered pleasantly on the other side of the wall, as if in the Garden of Eden. Soon, Grigori came to realize that just as legend tells of two different trees in paradise—one of the knowledge of good and evil, the other of eternal life—so too were there at least two mysterious residents or beings occupying the adjacent apartment.

First, there came indecipherable murmuring from behind the thin wall, after which someone bellowed so

loudly in Estonian that Cuffovich gave a start and hit
his head on the mirror hanging above the toilet.

"Who's that?" a woman demanded angrily in the
dead language. "Who's that?! The TV's on—go and
check, you goddamned asshole!"

Cuffovich rocked back on his heels and continued
listening in wonder—he'd learned Estonian at school
under the previous regime. The speakers appeared to
be a married couple, though he couldn't hear the man's
voice at all.

"Blah, blah, blah," the woman mocked. "Why can't
you ever remember anything, huh? If you can't understand or remember anything, then get the hell away
from the TV!"

How could anyone bear cohabitation under such
fusillades of cursing? Estonians . . . did they all act that
way? Lyuba had never chided him—she had merely
busied herself with her bears and crystal and grown
more and more distant over time. So distant, in fact,
that Grigori watched the transformation with childish
awe, like a kneeling Russian Orthodox priest who is
suddenly unable to find the right page and chapter in
the scripture, flip through it as much as he may. Grigori
decided that from now on, he must take the aggres-
sive neighbor-woman's words to heart; he must do his
best to consider them and find the deeper meaning of
life and existence. He carefully closed the door behind
him and walked to the city center at a leisurely pace.
Squinting from the corner of his eye, he perceived with
excruciatingly painful clarity how Viljandi had become

totally unfamiliar. It was not an intriguing difference that provoked curiosity, but rather a gentle and rising panic; something akin to what he'd felt when he'd gotten lost on vacation in Bukhara and ended up in front of an old-town post office packed with Tajiks. It was the sensation probably experienced by someone who leaves the house very seldom; a strange Little Muck whose only goal in life is the smoke rising from his chimney once per day. Truly, all that was missing were rascals lobbing stones; all that was missing were clothes too long for him and which kept getting caught under his shoes! Grigori was especially horrified by the frost-cloaked trees in the city center, whose branches seemed almost to be applauding the final act of his life's performance, upon which the final curtain was falling. Finally arriving at the Rainbow lake restaurant, he slumped wearily on the sofa by the kitchen door and hastily downed three strong Latvian beers without even knowing why. Before long, a disreputable businessman from the construction industry sat down beside him. This unpleasant character was currently working on a site with a dangerously gaping roof and strips of plastic sheeting that flapped loudly in the winter wind that howled among the girders. He was extremely disgruntled, because that day in the hairdresser's salon where he always got a free haircut (a business situated in the aforementioned neglected building), the woman had indignantly refused to provide her services, pointing to a fresh crack in a corner of the ceiling. This peremptory human judgement had astounded the businessman, a Mason and head of a large family, because he was someone who strove to put off divine judgement as long as he could. The businessman requested "The Rain Cries as it Shakes Its Long Coat" from the boys in the band and ended up dancing alone in the foyer like a melancholy, immigrant stork.

In the morning, Katerina awoke Grigori with kisses; she had already taken a shower and had a large towel wrapped around her head. Compared to life with Lyuba, an Estonian rationality and sense of eastern solicitousness permeated his new home; the sandwiches made in its kitchen had been kept warm since time immemorial. Katerina's nurturing was so intense that it felt as if the entire haul of the gold robbery that had not long ago shaken the small town had been dumped there in that tiny apartment next to the opera house—so exuberant and determined was the care lavished on Grigori, as if on stolen treasure. Even his job at the Rainbow felt increasingly foolish and unacceptable.

Grigori paid another visit to the toilet. The nice, warm little room with its striped wallpaper acted as an amazing amplifier of sounds emanating from outside its walls; it was a mysterious music box. Since he'd brought very few items from home and Katerina had immediately stored *them* in some attic *kamorka*, Grigori was delighted to have a new toy. For the first time, he grasped the accuracy of the clichéd belief that you don't require much in this life. His closet full of suits had been left behind, sinking into the throes of death and ultimate disuse. All he had in his new home was one suit jacket—just like in primary school—and one necktie; still, a man cannot wear more than that at one time. Life's hangars could snap beneath a heavy burden, but if the closet door was shut tight, then things weren't at all as bad as one might believe. The swishing of the falling clothes of Grigori's former life was less and less muffled in his ears. Thus, he brought a tin cup into the toilet the better to hear the snippets of wisdom coming from the Garden of Eden. How little he now needed to secure happiness! The painting of the bear cubs perched stiffly on their tree stumps and the crystal forest in the chestnut dusk of the sideboards, all of which Lyuba had purchased, now felt strange and distant. His former home was shut tight behind tourmaline cupboard doors.

Sitting on the toilet more or less as God had created him, Grigori pressed a tin cup against the wall in order to draw from the waters of eternal life behind it. That moment, he vividly recalled in all its terrible glory the legendary trick question often posed during theological seminars, which Noelhard's teacher (the old mystic Fail) had always loved to ask, specifically: Why had man been driven out of paradise in the first place? An angel carrying a flaming sword had been stationed at the gates as a guardian of wisdom and to keep man away from its sacred source, because those miserable garden residents had gotten out of hand and eaten from the tree of the knowledge of good and evil, and if they'd bitten from fruit of the other tree growing in paradise—that of eternal life—then man would have been equal to the gods. Therefore, God had sent them out into the bleak world and given them clothes of skin, resilient motorcycle

leathers, lest they scrape themselves as they slipped and
fell in life. Nevertheless, here was Grigori again, with his
tin cup, at the very gates of paradise, back at the beginning of ages and wisdom, his sole desire being to listen
and to think. His heart was pounding, the birds were
singing, and the TV was on, but no one spoke. Then,
suddenly, someone gave a long, evil, hiccupping, laugh,
making Grigori start and retreat to the kitchen in fright.

A few days later, Katerina asked Grigori to help a
neighbor shovel snow. Once he'd worked his way to the
corner of the building, he saw there was nothing behind
the toilet/music box whence the intriguing sounds had
emanated! There was no adjacent apartment, none at
all! There was nothing but a snow-caked outside wall
with two bare trees poking out of the powder. Grigori
laid his hand upon the wall—it was old, worn, and
charred, with a bricked-up doorway in the middle.
How could this be? Confused, disappointed, he went
back inside. There was no way the sounds could have
been real! His leaving Lyuba had had a severer effect
than he'd thought! Brushing the snow off his pants and
boots, he seated himself on the toilet, holding his head
between trembling hands. The sounds started up immediately: they struck him like a direct hit from a billiard
cue! Oddly enough, four Jewish rabbis had now chosen
that modest corner of the snowy yard on the other side
of the wall to hold a discreet conference! One could
imagine them sitting in the snow, their legs awkwardly
drawn up beneath their gored coats!

First of all, one of the elderly savants coughed for

several seconds before displaying to the others a crumbling pass allowing free tram rides, to a chorus of kvetchy *oy vey's*. It was the type of ordinary old-fogey talk commonly heard on the metro. But then, the men turned to an utterly mysterious topic.

"Hear my words," began the ticket-fantasy fogey, whom the others called Rabbi Akiva. "I know of your plans, but I do not approve of them and have come to warn you, though I naturally intended to stop by the market on the way. *Koroche*, as we know, there are two gardens of Eden: an upper one for souls and a lower one, where Adam resided with his first wife, Lilith. As you may recall from Jewish lyceum, Lilith, the first woman, was wiser than the world's first man and surpassed him in every way. Thus, another, more modest woman was created for Adam: Eve, who was made from his body, from his rib bone. Alas, the poor man longed for his first golden-haired beauty till the end of his days! And you, the Aristotles of Viljandi, you now fancy you are prepared to force your way into such a laboratory of God? Into the Shekhinah and Hekhalot? Into that world of mystical femininity and crystal palaces of the sky? And what's more, you hope to return *home* from there? To Viljandi and your porcelain figurines and little Mainas and Zinas on Jews Street? After such a kiss from Moses ?"

A pipe gurgled. Grigori pressed his ear harder against the tin cup.

"I will not come to place a stone upon your grave if you act like such fools! I will not go a second time

to steal the angel's flaming sword so that I can once
again barter for your return, you confounded Fausts of
Viljandi! Do you truly not grasp that man *must* die with
a sense of longing?!"

Frost crept into Grigori Cuffovich's soul as he listened. He recalled a cautionary tale about four rabbis
who journeyed to paradise. Only one returned: Rabbi
Akiva, the others having met their demise or gone insane.
The old Jewish story was not allegorical; rather, it was to
be taken as a frank warning against entering a strange
world unprepared. And wasn't that wise old man talking
about him *specifically* in his oy-vey-tramburay *skazka*
just now? Hadn't he himself ventured to the Promised
Land, where unearthly kisses drifted in the air? He had
rushed from his home, leaving all behind. Yet, wasn't
man's life merely a period of Egyptian slavery, during
which he must plant at least one tree in the Garden
of Eden and build one pyramid? Hadn't he renounced
everything too thoughtlessly; in too much of a zefiric jazz
rhythm? Indeed, he now regretted his actions. The world
went dark around him and he could see nothing but his
darling Lyuba.

All of a sudden, the toilet door was thrown open
and like a snowy rose bush, Rabbi Akiva stood before
Grigori in a long south-Estonian frock coat. The phantom extended its arm, even dripping snow into the small
metal bucket where the toilet paper was kept. Grigori
suddenly found himself outside in the snow and could
hear several men crying out as they fled. It was not the
old Jew murmuring prayers before him, whose voice,

which droned like a radio presenter's, Grigori Cuffovich unmistakably recognized as belonging to Rabbi Akiva from the other side of the wall! Rather, it was the other rabbis fleeing down the icy street! The whole world swam before Grigori's eyes and he could barely keep his balance. Next, he was flung into a giant hall where the angel Metatron sat upon a throne. That very moment, Grigori lost his faith in God the Creator, because he beheld someone else seated on the throne of paradise. An unhealable wound furrowed his spirit and soul.

Yet, he was already being propelled onward by a colossal force like a deadly illness; onward into Hekhalot, which was so cozy and nice that he regarded it as home for a moment. This was a fateful mistake, however, because the space around him suddenly roused itself with a shattering sound and snorted like a gigantic warhorse! Grigori was barely able to cling to the saddle. A shard of the palace wall—the horse's sharp crystal rib—sliced into his leg, leaving behind a piece of him forever. Something truly physical and earthly also had to be left behind in paradise.

Then, Rabbi Akiva fixed his gaze on the entire world and Grigori was back at the door to his old home. Standing next to him were two suitcases that looked as if they'd never been opened in his new home. He lifted his guitar case from the snow and began climbing the steps. An empty blue taxi was driving away down the cleared street in the gathering blizzard; Grigori realized he was holding change in his hand for some reason.

Waiting for him at the door to the apartment was his former wife Lyuba, his eternal Shekhinah, who kissed the returning man on the forehead like Moses and helped him inside.

The old hag in the third-story apartment, however, who had been peeking out between the curtains at the strange blue taxi and its female driver, was astonished the next morning to find that overnight, during the ash-blizzard, someone had impossibly planted two evergreen trees of an unknown variety directly beneath her bedroom window. The trees were also noticed by the ambulance paramedics who, early the next morning, transported Grigori Cuffovich Cuff to the insane asylum on the outskirts of the city.

Grigori Cuffovich's Crisis

Grigori awoke in a strange unfurnished space where motes of ash drifted in the air and naked old men slept strewn around the floor. Someone was snoring just like Noelhard! Grigori was in a terrible state; his head ached and his eyes itched. After a brief scuffle, he managed to slip out through the door with no handle and run down a flight of stairs to the toilet, when the caretaker had propped it open with a block of firewood to wheel in the patients' meal cart. The toilet was simply a fetid, gaping hole in the floor, but Grigori merely pressed his ear against the wall and listened. Sounds echoed all through the building: a caretaker was plodding down the stairs, someone was groaning somewhere, the janitor was sweeping outside. But then, birds began to chirp and Grigori felt the icy wall become suddenly warm, as if an invisible hand were insulating the world with comforting deficit-item Styrofoam. Then, someone gave a strange hiccupping laugh and the sounds of Estonian-language revelry and kissing rang out. Terribly crooked white tiling that was meant to conceal a former flue creaked and crumbled, and contrary to every rule and law of nature, the bathroom's barred art nouveau window swung open. Not fully understanding his actions, Grigori climbed, fell, and sprinted with insane strength across the bleak wasteland in the direction of town. He felt like a cube of sugar on a crystal saucer, being licked alternately by two gigantic women: Lyuba and Katerina. In response, the next time he stumbled and fell painfully into a snowbank, he bit back at life, filling his mouth with ash-covered but refreshing snow.

The new onion dome and the golden Byzantine melon dome on the water tower glittered in the early rays of sunlight. Even the new sixteen-story apartment blocks in the distant Männimäe neighborhood had swum off into the sea of light with the rising sun goddess. The sole dissonant note in the whole postcard-perfect morning was the spire of St. John's Church, which had dangled like a crane jib ever since the wartime fires. Grigori was still free, against all odds! However, an unknown hand had apparently written bad news for him on the back of that new day, because the blinds in every window of Katerina's apartment were shut tight and the doorbell had been disconnected. Grigori ran around the building and pounded on all of the windows, but no one came to open them. Finally, he craned his neck to peer at an angle through the side of the kitchen window . . . and was stunned. Sitting at the table with his back to Grigori was an unfamiliar gray-haired man, for whom Katerina was devotedly frying up cutlets! The stranger had wrapped Grigori's blue woolen sweatshirt around himself—it was draped in somewhat careless, Caucasus style over the intruder's shoulders, creating a sea of uncomfortable folds/volutes/creases in the fabric, as if a large child had pulled it on in a hurry and against his will.

So, Katerina had someone else! It dawned upon Grigori that all his attempts to create shared harmony with the woman had fallen flat! His grand efforts and departures from Lyuba's apartment had been for naught. How precious Lyuba now seemed with her crystal and her bears! Why, oh why had he left home? What sort of supernatural *kvakushka* had suddenly transformed him, an honest musician, into an Odessa-like character from a *feuilleton* who must sing to himself all alone in some tiny bar till the end of his days? The force had turned him into a sadly crackling Bulgarian microphone; an accordion's final chord; a philharmonic society's empty buffet!

His entire being now consisting of melting sugar, he collapsed in the snow next to a stack of firewood and put up no resistance when the blue taxi came to transport him through the bright sunshine back to the asylum. He wasn't even amazed to have the same pretty female driver, who wore a scuffed leather jacket, with a Nagant revolver at her waist. The woman's expression was slightly weary, but delicate. She spoke of love as she opened the door of the blue taxi, on whose seats gloomily blossomed bluish liverworts.

Departure from Paradise

The nighttime Viljandi tram was running at its normal speed on its usual route, but the doors did not open at the stops. The vehicle did make a brief stop in an unusual location: next to the market tobacco shop, where Murka Goldhand was making a quick *papirosa* cigarette purchase. Which is to say, she was buying one pack while a second . . . but that is of no consequence right now! There's an old saying and a song to the effect that a thief's romance is short but fiery. Murka, a full-fledged member of the criminal underworld, had already sacrificed today's workday at the market when she noticed Opiatovich napping in the passing tram and realized that there really did exist some sparks of amnesty in the stove! The grand authority was fast asleep in the danger zone! Perhaps he should go one step further and simply write his address on the soles of his boots? Luckily, the other members of the *shayka* quickly arrived. There they were: Caesar, Butterball, and Murderer, Armenian cognac still sloshing in their veins. The tram couldn't just be left standing there and none of the *shayka* were able to rouse Opiatovich, consequently, the situation had to be resolved by a straight dash in handcuffs, so to say: Caesar threatened the driver with his sharpened screwdriver while Butterball and Murderer behaved in such a way as to send the passengers scattering in a panic. Murderer chewed on a plastic water bottle as if it were a sweet glass-covered *pryanik*. The only thing sweeter than a *pryanik* is freedom! The riders hurried out of the tram car accordingly.

Caesar grabbed an imitation birch-trunk vase of artificial flowers. Swinging uncomfortably close to his cap was a souvenir monkey that dangled from the large rearview mirror, rhythmically attempting to plant a kiss on him with its puffy bright-red lips. Caesar felt as foolish as a brawny stevedore selling miniature chocolate drops in a candy store. The tram driver, a poor, trembling, little man, naturally did everything demanded of him without delay. For him, the lawless night-tram timetable now simply entailed driving through this moonbathed world without stopping.

As the tram careened down the market slope into Valuoja Valley, darting past the brand-new Khrushchyovka apartment blocks for the nomenklatura, only to ascend with unabated momentum toward the Russian Orthodox Monastery of the Paala *Gorodok* after passing the local Kronstadt luxury-zero, Opiatovich awoke and calmly surveyed his surroundings. Murka was standing before him, smoking. One couldn't say she was a beauty; rather, she was an uninspiring-looking female pickpocket who had showed up in Viljandi just recently. Her arrival had brought a great deal of trouble with it, because she operated alone. She was a true talent in the area of jewelry stores in particular, and appeared capable of undergoing complete transformations, becoming now a helpless pregnant woman, now the wife of an influential, renowned psychiatrist. Murka's magic theater was planned down to the finest detail for her various swindles, from wax-coated heels for embedding dropped pearls to a monkey that had been trained discreetly to swallow gems from a shop counter, before bravely enduring an emetic back at home. Murka wished to write her own dialogues in life and fully dissolve herself in the roles she played. Still, she hadn't managed to get by entirely without outside assistance: once, she employed Caesar and Butterball to act as police officers who had come to arrest her while shopping for diamonds. It was no coincidence that during the ensuing mayhem, several precious stones happened to scatter across the floor but were afterward impossible to find again! It was believed that only love could make Murka careless and be her Achilles heel, but so far, she hadn't strayed down that slippery slope. On the contrary! Just recently, she'd won fame and gravitas in the criminal world by way of a method she personally called "*guten morgen, fascist.*" While staying in a hotel, she would enter other rooms in the darkness of night to steal items, naked, and if she was caught . . . well, it goes without saying that no complaints were filed.

Opiatovich stared out the tram window with calm

curiosity. He'd never worked these stops, never ventured from the market toward the Paala *Gorodok*, as there were too many blue-striped state security workers and *militsiya* officers hurrying home. He preferred the cemeteries and parks that extended from the other side of the market, with their old ladies and mourners. Even more intriguing to Opiatovich, however, was the young thief. He was familiar with her story in broad outline: Murka had tracked him down as soon as she arrived in Viljandi, acknowledging his authority and asking his permission to glide independently through the world of gems like an invisible golden sediment. She showed respect.

It took just one look from Opiatovich for Caesar and Butterball to exit the tram in front of the Paala *Gorodok* Department Store. The man of his word had returned, his weakness had passed. Soon, the tram came to a switch where the tracks diverged.

"To the asylum or the theater?" asked Murka, rummaging through her purse for appearance's sake (it was actually empty). Opiatovich offered no reply. Still, he realized that even though there was no wisdom, no *nauka*, to be acquired from a broad like her, he had found himself in a defenseless position that day and she had helped him.

"I need to get to the Russian Theater; it's almost the intermission," remarked Murka, to put an end to the silly silence, leaning in toward the driver. Smirking, she pointed the way. All that could be seen ahead were snowy expanses and the distant light of the Glassmaker's Bar flickering in the blizzard like a Russian fairy tale.

Opiatovich lifted his gaze and stared unblinkingly at the woman framed by the cheap window of the tram manufactured at the Krakow Machine Factory. He felt as if his whole life to date had been pointless—some strange fever enveloped him after his vision-filled night. A great magnet was pulling him toward love; heat suddenly filled each and every blood cell, driving out any shred of logic!

"Murka, kitty—you wouldn't want to marry me, would you?"

It was the most illogical thing the old pickpocket had ever uttered. Whereas thitherto Murka might have thought the respected man-of-his-word had been struck by some kind of old-timer's illness, now . . . he should probably have taken the opposite direction from the theater—the direction of the hospital and Jämejala Asylum . . .

"A thief never marries because the state gives the stamp," Murka answered curtly. Her eyes were trained on the crowd waiting at the next stop. The tram screeched to a halt and its doors opened.

"One ticket to the Russian Theater, please," Opiatovich heard a gruff voice demand. It belonged to a man of conspicuous affluence; the cuffs of his coat, and even his bowtie, were made of expensive fur. Astonishingly, Murka, who just a moment earlier had been pensive and still, had undergone a great transformation. She was emitting heartbreaking sobs from a seat reserved for the elderly and disabled, whereupon the wealthy citizen immediately went to console her.

They alighted together at the next stop, the man trustingly holding his arm beneath that of the talented Murka. Opiatovich changed trams to head in the opposite direction, back toward the asylum's high-fenced grounds on the other side of Valuoja Park's thick woods. After alighting from the tram, he stopped and squatted at the barbwire gate. Opiatovich could see no other solution: he had to enter a place of incarceration once more and start polishing himself. There was no longer any freedom in freedom—a devil-knows-what kind of boundless game was underway in the town and a cryptic force was wreaking havoc; a damned, Gogol-like curse! He wasn't quite inclined to return to imprisonment voluntarily, of course, but he needed a program to restore his character and to do it fast; the insane asylum seemed like a reasonable option. Before long, Opiatovich was noticed and ushered inside. The critical moment, the dark element, and love's hot porridge were routine phenomena inside.

Cutlets for Gogol

Katerina had been alone downstairs the entire day, crying over Grigori's disappearance. She finally composed herself and went back to work around midnight (in spite of Opiatovich having forbidden her to do so), where she discovered the bar door ajar and Gogol asleep in the moonlight in the park at the intersection. She went quickly inside to tidy up, then borrowed a wheelbarrow from the courthouse yard across the street. The building's exotic, ethnic Estonian janitor primarily used it to collect the shards of red tile that fell from the disintegrating roof. Katerina then determinedly wheeled the conspicuously-dressed Gogol back to her home. Late-night smokers loitering outside the nightclub directed catcalls at her and her load, but she was accustomed to obstreperous bargoers and paid them no heed. Gogol had to be taken somewhere safe. The horrendous cobblestones that the new tsardom had pounded into place during its very first days in power jolted the wheelbarrow, so Katerina removed her soft rose-patterned shawl and positioned it under the moaning Gogol's back.

At home, she started making cutlets in the early-morning gloom—more to soothe her own nerves than out of hunger. Katerina had placed high hopes in Grigori. He had promised her the Sun and the Moon and even moved into her place, but now he had disappeared all the same, and had done so in such a rush that he hadn't even flushed the downstairs toilet! Grigori had spent an odd amount of time in the bathroom in general, and even took a cup along with him, as if he intended to drink the toilet water! Good Lord! Maybe he had some strange disease? Bloody urine? It was a shame that everything had gone the way it did, of course . . . but on the bright side, at least *some* male soul had entered her house again! Furthermore, Katerina had an inexplicable affection for the taciturn prophet—Gogol had eaten his meals at the Novel ravenously and had spoken words that went straight to her heart; had uttered long-awaited answers to her great questions. And he never used awful threefold idioms! Katerina felt an unfathomable thrill and dignity. For some reason, a certain pop song kept playing in her head, about a beautiful woman who lived in a riverside house, beneath which a crystal-clear stream started trickling one fine day. She was also reminded of the Gospels—in the end, only women had remained at the foot of the Redeemer's cross, because all the men fled!

The cutlets turned out fantastically. The great Gogol

ate sedately and in silence, like an old engraving come to life, which suddenly appears to move when glimpsed by a late-night bathroom-goer in the wrong light. When Katerina offered him wine, the stranger pointed to the kettle and had her pour him a glass of hot water. She noticed that he had the unusual habit of molding his bread into pellets. What's more, all the windows and mirrors in the apartment had to be covered. When they arrived and the woman gave the shivering Gogol a sweatshirt Grigori had left behind, the prophet stared out into the darkness of night for a long time, muttering that carriages used to turn around in front of his previous abode, perpetually splattering the window with mud. Gogol tugged at the blinds and Katerina granted his strange wish, proceeding to close all of them. When the bloodied and clearly deranged Grigori showed up at the house, a neighbor made the call to the asylum. All Katerina could do was watch from the balcony above as the man from whom she had expected so much was taken away in a blue taxi. Growing cold, she went back inside to sit and nap next to the sleeping Gogol, not having the slightest clue how to move on with her shattered life. After a while, Katerina awoke and placed her hands upon the man—his arms were as cold as ice and his face was covered in tiny lacerations probably inflicted when the cast of his death mask was taken; wounds the woman hoped to disinfect in the morning with some good Yugoslavian spikenard oil. Gogol woke up once during the night and, in a semi-somnambulant state, tried to clamber upstairs to where he claimed the home chapel was! The visitor likewise howled in his sleep a couple of times, calling out for his servant, but having exhausted himself, fell back into a deep sleep. After breakfast, Gogol decided to spend the day in the toilet as was his wont, and Katerina did not deny this bizarre request—where else should a dead man be? She even brought him a few ballpoint pens and some scraps of notebook paper. A couple of Estonian-language literary works—*Rise and Shine* by an older author named Jan Kaos and a thick book titled *Tartu Title Track* by the Estonian-Nigerian Nobel Prize winner Berk Vakri—were resting on a birch-wood shelf in the toilet for non-reading purposes, in accordance with the imperial decree on Estonian literature: specifically, at least two works on the official list were to be kept in areas designated for hygiene at all times. Luckily, Gogol said they were too complex for him . . . Katerina didn't want any trouble. She lived a quiet life and always abided by state laws; they were so ingrained in her that she mentally weighed her homemade cutlets in tsarist grams and, it goes without saying, strictly adhered to the "blue decrees" that regulated relationships with any remnants or representatives of former Estonian statehood.

Katerina had invited a guest to come over the next evening. Her friends were truly her sole joy in life. The dearest of them—Katya—worked as the director of two factories located quite far apart from each other, so she called on her soul-sister frequently, if only for the purely practical benefit of having a place to stay for the night. Nevertheless, Katerina's intoxicating anticipation had dissipated with the unexpected development. She had not yet told Katya about Gogol and intended to serve the bombshell on a cart that could be "wheeled in," so to say, but as always, something started burning in the kitchen at the busiest possible moment. Katya was left alone in the entryway. Her shrill scream rang out almost immediately, as she discovered the skeletal old man from beyond the grave reading mandatory toilet literature in the bathroom. Such books were stocked everywhere by law, but no one ever *picked them up*! Katya felt as if she were going to die a gruesome death that very day on a park bench, not far from which a committee of local thieves was convening in the bushes that dotted the eerie ruins of Castle Hill—so terrible was that phantom! The repulsive and illegal act of reading an Estonian book in the toilet was so unconscionable that the strawberry cake she'd bought from the confectionary slipped from her fingers and smashed on the ground with a *plop*.

Nevertheless, calm was gradually restored, and life's unexpectedly hot broth cooled down when Katerina later asked the stranger to emerge and, clad in raspberry-red pants, Gogol, with trembling gallantry, offered the women unfiltered cigarettes from his squeaky cigarette case. Katya knew Katerina had always possessed a kind of elusive, hidden style; probably as a result of her Baltic heritage. With this friend by her side, the situation was so much more exciting—Katya had never encountered such a fascinating man at her factories. Not even the IT guy was on par with Gogol, though he also dressed bizarrely and spoke only in gibberish. Katya stared in wide-eyed wonder as Katerina took her most treasured ointment from the bedroom and rubbed it on the old man's legs. The room filled with a pungent, churchy aroma. Katya inspected the packaging and was left dumbstruck—it cost almost her annual salary. Katerina's hair brushed against the ointment every time she leaned over Gogol, but she didn't care. For a moment, it even appeared as if her dear friend was using her hair to wipe the phantom's brown, rotting feet. Lastly, Katerina applied the ointment to Gogol's face, probably to treat the cuts made by his death mask.

"Why on earth are you using such an expensive ointment on him?" Katya asked as soon as she and Katerina were alone together in the kitchen. "You can't live with an old geezer like him, you know, he won't bring home the bacon . . . How about a long-distance trucker, instead? I could arrange it; I've told you before . . ."

Katerina sat down at the kitchen table and burst into tears.

"Look, he's only going to be here a little while, but those other men are around all the time," she sighed when she composed herself. "I just started feeling sorry for him—he's a total *nemodny*-parasite-*unitaz*, of course, but Grisha upped and left, and I don't have it in me to start . . ."

"Yes, but you really can't live with somebody like him, Katerinka," Katya insisted, her face now fully illuminated by the inner lamp of female astonishment. "You could feed an ordinary man for three-hundred-odd days with the money from that ointment! He's no Christ, now is he?! And we're not Jewish women! On top of that, if the inspectors show up and catch him reading, then no one will be able to protect you anymore—you'll be an *Estonka*. Do you want to be hauled off to the old metro tunnels to die, too?"

"The metro!" Katerina exclaimed. "I've been an honest servant of the tsardom my whole life—I've never even read *newspapers* in the toilet . . ."

She wept like a prostitute or train-station pianist. Oh, how she needed a Grigori in her life, a little *aranzhirovchik* of everyday affairs who would tell her what was right and wrong and what the point of life was; who would set the right atmosphere and always pull just the right amount of cash out from under the piano cover! Her whole life was a mess yet again—like Pskov's France Boulevard after its opening ceremony.

Katya tried to think in a businesslike way for a moment, just like at the factory whenever the workmen came to gripe about not having one thing or another. On those occasions, she'd usually have them display their tools to her, after which they'd realize there were actually no grounds for demanding anything extra and that all the right conditions for drudgery had indeed been met. Katya attempted to formulate her developing standpoint:

"There must be some place safer and better for him. There's nothing wrong with your place, of course— it's worlds beyond a communal apartment; that goes without saying. But listen, Katerinka: what if we were to take him to the museum?"

Katerina stood there, her eyes glinting oddly, like a house's last nightlight flung in a pond.

"Yes!" she declared after a minute's silence, her voice cracking.

The women gathered their wits about them and returned to the living room. Gogol had withdrawn to the toilet again and all the bread on the table had been rolled into pellets. The two friends quietly began packing what they would need.

At Badenov's

Arkasha opened his left eye; he'd been unconscious for several hours. Straight away, he recognized Badenov's room, packed with musical artefacts, and farted in relief. What on earth had *that* been? What confounded vision had overcome him in the toilet of the Armenian restaurant? A geisha-stool-baby?! Not even a carnival director could come up with anything sillier—it was utter foolishness in the style of I-came-to-your-club-to-the-carnival-the-waltzing-couples-are-swimming!

The walls of Badenov's room flooded him with a sense of security. Once, long ago, when he'd paid a visit to this very space and casually started singing out of boredom, Badenov—Baddy—had helped usher him into the world of vaudeville. Oh, the looks on their faces when they burst into the room, that Vasya-Beatles-man and Badenov! They immediately proposed to record his cracking baby's voice and stupid jokes on X-ray films so that the whole nation might have a chance to sympathize with his highway-rose-scented wounds!

His lyricism and songs about war and Odessa sold like gold. All that remained to be done was to find good bandmates to accompany him. Once, a saxophonist had smoked himself to such a char during a recording that he kept blaring intermittently and ultimately had to be tied down to the drums! Oh, the times and those musical trams that had been set rolling along concert tracks with Badenov's production, unfiltered cigarettes rolled from sheet music burning sweetly in both their mouths! You could hear the clinking of kopecks as soon as the cigarette burned the hole in the middle of the X-ray record! People were ravenous for that thrill of notes-on-bones! The official variety singers were no good—the *chansons* and the *blatnyaki* were what imparted such fame that every taxi driver in the small town would shove cash and cognac bottles into your pockets, ferrying you from one bar to another.

Upon noticing that Arkasha, his foundling and *blatnoy-stilyaga-jazzmanchik*, had woken up, Badenov hurried into the communal kitchen to make tea. It was a good thing he had finally come to his senses—carrying the man all the way home from the bar had been worth the effort! While searching for the kerosene stove, he heard Arkasha take his old guitar down from the wall and start plucking away. His condition had apparently improved! Saint Mary of Egypt be praised! Badenov shook his head and adjusted his pants. It was absolutely baffling! Some terrible force had made itself known to Arkasha, just like the horror that washes over a lone singer who hums a gypsy tune in the milky moonlight and suddenly hears a snickering, gypsy greeting from the darkness. "We managed to get him all the way here from the nightingale's bar—let him feel at home like an exotic avocado or a criminal *Mikado*; let him rest," reckoned Badenov. On the other hand, a contradictory impulse was drifting through his mind—a plan worthy of a true counter admiral. Specifically, if Noelhard wasn't around (and indeed, he wasn't—he and his van had disappeared completely), they could hold a proper apartment concert down at the bookstore and make a pretty kopeck off Arkasha's songs! Time and again, he'd proposed such an opportunity to Noelhard, but the bookstore owner was wary of others; was afraid the shady types drawn to the place—the whole gamut of waiters and taxi drivers— would make off with his books and chunks of shungite. Oh, dearie me! Who on earth wanted those bits of black Karelian gravel, anyway! All kidding aside, though: what if he were to throw a little concert? Badenov started frying an egg to let himself think and calm his nerves.

Meanwhile, Arkasha was looking around the room in bliss. For some reason, it'd been ages since Badenov had invited him up! Only greenish shadows were visible through the tall, oblong window, as Castle Street was narrow and lined by multi-story buildings pressed tightly together like in a metropolis! *Pling-pling!* Two accordions hung side-by-side beneath an enormously long shelf of vinyl records that divided the wall. Stacked in a corner were several old speakers and unwashed, wine-stained mugs left over from a long-ago party. Crisscrossing the ceiling were innumerable cords, along with record covers and posters of various denim-jeaned bands. A couple failed attempts at Vysotsky portraits had been heaved onto an old wardrobe with a mirrored door, and the wardrobe itself was filled with . . . reel-to-reel tapes! There was even a shelf specially constructed beneath the window from rough boards with yawning gaps between them, which Badenov used for storing old record players. Some were apparently kept running at all times like living history—they whispered and flickered in the dark like deep-sea *ryba*.

"Here you go," said Badenov, entering the room with the frying pan. "Take an egg." He carried the pan strangely, as it had no handle, holding it by the edges like an expensive foreign record.

Arkasha ate. Close to one hundred little musician figurines—some made of porcelain or clay, others of wood, the majority naturally being plastic—watched him from a shelf. Enthroned in the center of the throng was a giant alarm clock, from which an inexplicable cord ran across the room to disappear behind a shelf, suspended in the air like a nighttime tram line. The most unusual item in the room, however, was a rather large statue of a Dalmatian in one corner, which stared sadly at the ceiling amid all those musical artifacts. No doubt the dust-*laik-laika* dog was pondering good and bad music or black and white jazz.

"Tell me, what on earth happened to you?!" Badenov asked softly.

Arkasha stopped chewing. His jaw hung open and a strange flame kindled in his eyes.

"What are you . . . quit it!" Badenov mumbled, and helped feed his friend fried egg with a spoon. Arkasha was staring in terror at the souvenir club with polished spikes that hung on the wall.

Badenov sat on the narrow bed and folded his arms pityingly. In truth, he was already calculating the possible profits a performance by Arkasha, the national bard, would bring in at Noelhard's bookstore. He'd have to get more chairs from somewhere, that much was clear—the taxi drivers certainly wouldn't want to sit on the wooden floor.

"I've had no luck in life. Some old memories were reawakened—I might have a kid from a long time ago," Arkasha sighed, staring mournfully at the empty pan. It symbolized his whole life, which had no handle, either.

He hauled himself to his feet and looked around the clammy museum-room.

"Mm-hmm . . . yeah . . ." he grunted.

Arkasha thought hard. "I collapsed in the restaurant. My friend Badenov took me home. What's so unusual about that?!" His belly was nice and full now, in any case. He sighed and started looking for his plastic bag. Screeching light from the streetlamp spilled in through the window.

"Stay the night," said Badenov, taking a bottle of vodka off a cupboard and setting it on the table.

Arkasha nodded. He rolled up his sleeves and filled two glasses. Then, Badenov started to discuss his concert plan.

"Oh-ho-ho . . . let's do it!" Arkasha, who resembled

a little sparrow, finally confirmed with flashing eyes. He was already reveling in the thought of making and splurging money when he suddenly remembered the events of the previous day and was overcome by fear and disgust. They agreed to hold the concert the very next day, as otherwise, Noelhard might manage to interfere.

The rapidly-surfacing memories of what had transpired at the Armenian restaurant caused another shiver to run down Arkasha's spine, like a dangerous wave ebbing from Yalta beach. Toasty vodka-warmth flooded his body as he undressed and pulled a blanket over himself. He fell into a dead sleep with visions of concert-poster glue binding him to a drainpipe on a blustery street.

The Apartment Concert

An unbelievable crowd gathered at the bookstore the following night. One taxi driver yanked another by his leather jacket; after elbowing her way in, a woman promptly blocked the entryway, falling to her knees as if in prayer. Badenov collected ticket money and in the end spent almost fifteen minutes counting it, so great was the haul. More and more guests were still showing up on the snowy front steps. The street was jam-packed with vehicles, astounding even the taxi drivers, whose curiosity was particularly aroused by the unusual blue taxi that arrived with an unfamiliar female driver.

Arkasha was already bantering with the crowd. He'd climbed to the highest rung of the ladder and balanced his folder of song lyrics on the branches of the chandelier. Badenov flipped the light switch, blanketing the rest of the space in darkness and quiet. Arkasha's face swung in the circle of light as if under a circus tent. He switched to a tone simultaneously queer and solemn.

"Hello, friends. First of all, I'd like to talk a little

about *chansons* and *chansonettes*—you know, the bru-
nettes who've got no chance in life!"

The audience roared with laughter. There were all
kinds of characters present, to put it mildly. Seated on
two chairs in the front row (and strikingly out of place
in comparison with the rest of the ragtag crowd, like a
great syzygy of the planets) was the great and wealthy
conductor Osmo Vanska, wearing a gigantic signet ring.
He raised a hand, the ring glistened, and the crowd fell
silent. They understood; they obeyed! Having a mil-
lionaire-producer-gold-mask of such caliber show up
to hear little Arkasha meant the whole town could feel
a sense of pride without any further thought or discussion! Vanska's patent leather shoes surveyed everything around them like two plump, arrogant rats. On
his head, the distinguished guest was wearing a summer captain's cap, for some reason. Waiting by the door
and glaring with growing disdain at both the entering
guests and his own striped red pants, which were getting
colder by the minute, was the doorman of the luxury
Hotel London, who had accompanied Vanska to the
venue.

"So, friends, may you have freedom and bread and
living songs; those things, I wish for you! Our genre
today will extend back to folk songs and include the
repertoire of *shashlik*-prostitutes and card players. I
will sing twenty-one songs for you—may the Arkasha
show begin! Don't spit—otherwise, the Arab partisan
Muhammad Ali will show up and strike with all his
might, sending you flying right off life's pedestal!"

Arkasha started his performance with gypsy songs
that sent a ripple of snickers through the audience.
Next, and without any fluid transition, he launched
into the legendary ditty "The Oriental Café," in which
three women perform a striptease. Two whores did
start dancing somewhat provocatively at the foot of the
ladder, but were chastised by an older taxi driver who
resembled a plump bottle of port wine in a leather case.
Once Arkasha rasped out his real pop song (the message
of which was that Viljandi would always be cramped,
even if there were fifty of them), even gold signet ring
started to chuckle. Badenov realized the night was an
honest-to-goodness, bang-up, success, ah-cha-chaa!
Even a princess of Nepal or a lord of Edenborough
would have been satisfied with the show! Vanska was
enjoying himself, and the sweetest songs were yet to
come!

That was when Arkasha really got into the swing of
things! Wildly popular refrains were already booming
back from the audience, like the one about how every
woman in Viljandi is a poetess and understands the
men even before they start speaking, or the silly song
about a south-Estonian wedding where the chucklehead
groom starts counting the silver just as the party is getting underway. Still, the crowd descended into a true
frenzy only once Arkasha began belting out the prison
tunes with all their Shakshas, Alyoshas, sugarless jams,
beloved mothers, dry biscuits, and salty tears soaring
helter-skelter with storks and birch-patterned bars.

Arkasha was damp with perspiration, the audience

screaming in enthusiasm. Suddenly, the lights were switched back on and Butterball the criminal forced his way to the front of the crowd, muttering something about how those songs shouldn't be sung just anywhere or anyhow. Vanska raised his signet ring into the air and wearily declared: "Come now, boy, this Arkasha of yours is a genuine contra-natural-bandit . . ."

The crowd was intoxicated by the great conductor's great words and the little man's little melodic trickeries. The concert resumed! First, Arkasha howled a song about a calamitous woman who blows kisses as she enters the bar at the Viljandi Bus Station and ultimately allows the men to make her light up like a chandelier. Alas, some crooks start to quarrel, one whips out a *finka* and inflicts a mortal wound right below another's fifth rib bone.

Arkasha then started to wrap things up, moving on to a cycle of slower, emotional ballads. The plump Butterball made no further comment, instead casually starting to file the window grating.

Badenov's eyes sparkled with joy as he flicked through the bills—the best pages in the world! And the book of them he was holding was so thick! The door had remained blissfully shut for a while already; no one new had trickled in. Through the window, he could see the freezing hotel doorman, like a horse in an overcoat, still waiting loyally for Vanska to emerge from the awful lair. All of a sudden, Mr. Squall was standing before Badenov. He was wearing a greasy button-up vest that should have been banished from God's light long ago.

"What is it? What do you want?!" Badenov mumbled with a rising sense of dread. Mr. Squall's unbooted, sockless bare feet were purple from the cold; his sagging children's trousers had odd, old-fashioned stripes. Even from a rock-and-roll standpoint, the insane little Estonian was far too much to handle.

Mr. Squall giggled and produced a tiny mirror from his pocket.

"Allow me . . . Mister Badenov . . . yes-yes . . . much money! But if you were to look at it here in the mirror, it would double!"

Badenov took a deep breath. *Ptui* . . . Damn that Squall! His mind was occupied enough as it was. He suspected a glance into Squall's mirror would leave a cryptic mark on his soul. That damned Estonian ghost and his babbling!

"What do you want?" Badenov repeated, his eye starting to twitch.

Squall merely dashed outside.

If anyone had pursued him, that deranged, curious soul would have found himself in the abandoned puppet theater across the street. Squall pounded up the stairs—darting to and fro was the only way he moved. Mumbling to himself, he searched for the key to the auditorium, but finally gave up and wormed his way in through the pet flap. The walls of the gigantic deteriorating space were packed with mirrors of all shapes and sizes, baroque-framed pieces and peasant rusticity side by side, and the only kind lacking were new store-bought specimens. They appeared to warp into a row of endless reflections like the spinning of the Vatican's eternal roulette wheel. Mr. Squall had arranged the puppets on the floor so as to capture nice reflections of their doll-families and groups. However, there was also a second and much more complicated system in place, for the puppets and pasteboard stage scenery were laid out in such a way as to trace the outlines of the old Estonia's county boundaries. Thus, in a sense, Mr. Squall had created the most forbidden phenomenon imaginable: an enormous map of the late Estonian state with all its Jõgeva and Valga and Võru municipalities! Toy trains stood between the cities. Bowls of foul water designated the larger bodies of water. Most of the puppets were covered with soiled bedsheets to signify they were deceased. Mr. Squall stretched out wearily on the floor, but was harassed by thoughts and disquiet; sleep would not come. Reality was being warped again somewhere, it seemed! He crawled to a table, from which he seized a hunting rifle. One puppet was still standing close to where he slept in his home county. A shot rang out and dust billowed! Mr. Squall crawled back and pulled the same sheet over himself. Now, almost everyone in the space was covered. Mr. Squall had entered his Viljandi.

"How can you blame me?" Badenov wondered with a sense of mild discomfort. Still, the pain was sweet because he'd collected a nice little mound of cash. "You can't say my life has been a fountain!"

The concert over, the floor was dotted with puddles. In one corner, Arkasha was chatting with a woman in a leather jacket. A detective? *Militsiya?* Sweat dripped into Badenov's eyes. A journalist would be no better, as such concerts were strictly prohibited, and he could find himself in a great deal of misery for many years if the ticket stubs were discovered. Soon, the stranger departed and Arkasha approached him, his eyes gleaming.

"Oy-oy, Vanska invited us to dine with him!"

Badenov mumbled a garbled response, brushing off the idea. So what? The great conductor might have been tippling again, et cetera.

"Are you sure?" he asked, his keen gaze surveying the scene. Quite a lot of books had tumbled off their shelves and, for some reason, whether because someone had been bored or whether because it was part of some greater scheme of things, the window grating had been sawn through. He pressed Arkasha about the identity of the woman, but the musician merely shrugged—she'd just politely asked for Noelhard.

At the Restaurant

The doorman stood in the foyer of the luxury Hotel London and started howling as soon as he spotted the men. Even the waiter in sparkling cuffs came out to see what was happening.

"They'll fling shit all over the walls if you let them in, damned *studyent-nemodnye*-illegals!" the latter proclaimed, not mincing words.

"They'll puke everywhere," chimed in the doorman, in solidarity, peering glassy-eyed at Arkasha and his torn, sweat-soaked jacket.

The foyer was dreadfully quiet. Real, genuine wax candles dripped from heavy gold candelabras. Badenov and Arkasha felt uncomfortable standing there, even though the rug was as soft as a fuzzy *pelmen* being licked by the sweet fate of Misha the Bear.

"Vanska's expecting us! Don't you recognize me? I'm Arkady! It's not like I've come here to marry you, you slaves!"

The doorman smirked and playfully shoved the waiter toward the restaurant.

"Well, go ahead and let the cholera on the tram, as they say; it's true, these crooks are Vanska's guests today."

"Coats first!" rasped Arkasha.

That moment, Vanska descended the staircase wearing a quilted bathrobe and slippers with golden pompoms. A table was set for him like magic and the vodka flowed profusely, the waiters multiplying constantly as if rising up from beneath the floor.

"Make yourselves at home! Don't worry, this is an awful, godforsaken dump, but all should be in abundance here today!"

Badenov dined on lamprey salad and cod liver, wiping his mouth with a white handkerchief that he pulled out of the condescending waiter's breast pocket. Oh, what a grab-me-anywhere-you-may, rock-and-roll atmosphere! As if he were Presley or Vysotsky! Life had a theme and tone! Opportunities glimmered like the Bay of Yalta . . . And today, money was like hot pebbles beneath your feet on the beach at Sochi!

"Why do you always show up so late?" Arkasha growled at the waiter in charge of vodka, who had already run himself out of breath. The men were on their fifth or sixth decanter.

"Now, tell me, Arkasha—our national talent," Vanska began, looking like an émigré-*biznesmen*-electric fireplace. His shirt was unbuttoned and his chest radiated the pure joy of burning cash. "Where are you from? Who are you?"

Arkasha began his story, accompanied by Vanska's rumbling grunts of approval. Badenov listened in fascination, as he actually didn't know all that much about his friend's earlier doings. First, the urban romancer told them about a place called Ivanovo, his childhood home, grasslands, wooden houses. He concluded the chapter by mentioning that a statue dedicated to him as a singer had been erected in the town. Badenov was breathless and eager as he immersed himself in the wild fantasy. The great Vanska became sentimental.

"Your temporal intonation is in the right place, my man," he interjected with his low bass.

From there, Arkasha moved on to his time at the Estonian Forest Institute and his fondness for trees; especially birches. He also brought up the secret passions of his student years and the frivolous literature he'd gone to borrow from Badenov on their first encounter. Vanska looked over at his friend, who nodded confirmation. It was all (or, well, *almost* all) correct. Memories are like rays of autumn sunlight, for which one is always glad. And everyone has them—even those whose profiles will never be minted on coins!

Arkasha then gave an overview of the war between Estonia and Imperial Russia, during which he had served in a helicopter regiment and even trained in Vietnam. By the time NATO was defeated and the tiny Baltic nation conquered, he'd held seven different passports and had officer's epaulettes on his shoulders!

Vanska ordered the lights to be lit on the tiny restaurant stage; reeling, Arkasha mounted the stage. The conductor was chuckling and perched on his chair like a director in the middle of the dancing grounds. The waiters had lined up respectfully and were watching like hypnotized rabbits.

Arkasha emitted a spirited shriek, then scratched his fingernails over the floorboards and launched into a ditty about a fried chicken! It was an insane song and he was apparently improvising additional verses. According to the story Arkasha told, a fried chicken was once arrested and asked for his passport. Vanska stomped his slippers on the wooden floor in delight! When it turned out the chicken had no passport, the officer asked for a coin! The chicken had no money, either, so it had to give up its coat. The song concluded with awful and very Arkasha-like baying about how chickens have a will to live, too; no matter if they're fried!!!

Vanska was dancing and bellowing vows to make Arkasha a global celebrity! He personally poured the performer a glass of champagne. They embraced. It was apparently after this that the great conductor asked the national talent a fateful question: whether there was anything he could give or gift the man. Arkasha looked around like a woman in the excruciating throes of childbirth and wondered what might aggravate the waiter-slaves the very most. Then, he uttered-stammered-gasped-spat out the portentous words: "Luxury is lacking; my soul yearns for something exceptional!"

The maestro beckoned to the maître d' and the doorman. The two wore perturbed expressions as they processed his whispered instructions, then disappeared.

Vanska stamped his food like God creating the world and collapsed into his chair.

"An entire museum will be brought here at once!"

"A museum?!" Badenov echoed in astonishment, scanning the space.

"A museum," the great Osmo Vanska confirmed with a nod.

The entire length of narrow Castle Street was thundering. Buildings shook with such intensity that it would have been better to reverse the lenses of every peephole so as not to be affrighted at the spectacle of what was underway! Crystal stars sprung into the sky and the standard state monument to the unknown, unmarked hero— the little green man—trembled like a hussar before a virgin maiden at a brothel! If an earthquake were to erupt while someone was having a bath, then the serene bather couldn't be blamed for leaping out of the tub in a panic, could he?! Mr. Squall awoke to mirrors crashing down around him. Stepping over the fallen puppets of Viljandi County, he used a stool to climb up onto the broad nineteenth-century windowsill. He was reaching for the latch when he froze in horror, like an outdoor thermometer struck by a woodpecker's beak. His very own Republic-era living room furniture was undulating past! The buffet cabinet he'd bought in Riga, the Biedermeier sofa, the tall grandfather clock—even his old birdiecage! Rolled-up rugs and palms poked up intermittently; his old copper dishes had been hung from the branches of his rubber fig tree, clattering and glinting in the moonlight like a Jewish Christmas tree. What was going on?! Then, a howling reached his ears! Was it another deportation? Several women were staggering through the snow behind two armored cars piled high with his possessions, wailing and screaming. Mr. Squall no longer cared about the details—he cared only for his things! He dashed to the furthest window, opened it, and leapt out onto his former possessions, sailing through the sky, rifle in hand! The familiar, musty scent of the cupboards was maddening, coaxing him into a gentle and überintimate inner cosmos.

The peculiar caravan didn't drive very far, shuddering over the Post Street intersection and coming to a stop in front of the red-brick Hotel London, like a funeral procession before a cathedral or a corpulent criminal smashing his fist down on the keys of a beer-soaked bar piano as he left. Doors were flung open, waiters shooed the women away, and to ensure his threats were taken seriously, the newer employee with a particularly shady past flashed his *finka*.

Vanska's merrymaking was undisturbed by the flurry of activity. The entire restaurant had acquired a new, maniacal appearance and now bore a greater resemblance to a gypsy caravan pitching camp in a professor's apartment! Villu, the legendary old glass-eyed waiter/ bouncer, felt like the olden days had returned; his nonexistent eye overflowed with nostalgia. Arkasha was no longer singing, but screaming like a true bandit with every ounce of his 90 pounds. He'd flung his shirt into a corner and now looked like a little glass swan, perfectly translucent in his madness.

The Death of the Temple Builder

Caesar, Butterball, and Murderer allowed the caravan to pass without taking any risks. Laying a finger on the trucks bearing the coat of arms of the town commander would be a senseless act, even in their dreams. Instead, they slunk into courtyard behind the bookstore and pried open the sawed grating in order to break in. Once, in his younger days, Butterball had even bent a giant tree down over a ditch while hiking through a swamp—he possessed the strength and *dukh* of several men. Alas, the bookstore was squalid and empty; there was certainly nothing of value left to take, and the cash register was empty. Only a small box of tools, which a pawn shop might consider taking, caught the thieves' eyes.

Noelhard's great longcase Gustav-Beckett-fascist-scareclock struck twelve awful chimes for midnight, and that's when it happened: someone else entered the bookstore. Annoyed, the men in the back room grabbed whatever they could find.

Vasya Kolyugin, his face snow-white after coming around from his severe narcotic high, materialized before the thieves like a ghost. Having risen from his stupor and lost any sense of time, the Beatlesman-temple builder-dreamer stood in the doorway and gaped at the intruders from beneath puffy brows. Caesar was the first to strike, having seized a tin plumb from Noelhard's toolbox. Although he aimed for Vasya's forehead, either the weapon proved unsteady or the surprise was so great that he hit Vasya's right temple instead, causing the victim to reel and fall to his left knee. Vasya then made a mad rush at his attackers and was dealt the next blow by Murderer, who swung Noelhard's spirit level against the man's left temple, sending him flying into a bookshelf and crushing his right knee. Seizing upon his last remaining chance, he attempted to crawl to the toilet, but was met there by the third villain, Butterball, who slammed a hammer into the dead center of his forehead. Vasya Kolyugin the Temple Builder fell dead at Butterball's feet. A cheap clay temple model shattered on a shelf, as if a golden beaker had fallen and splintered or a heavy windlass had tumbled into a well. Temple shards and fine glittering dust settled on the murdered Vasya as his soul entered on an unexpected meeting with Lennon.

Outside, a cat emitted a heartbreaking yowl. Butterball went to open the door, smirking. It was an old *blatnoy* trick. The men were caught off their guard and shot cruelly and suddenly by a Nagant revolver, like the infamous star rash striking a syphilitic father on a beautiful Sunday morning. All three killers fell.

The young woman covered the body in the back room with a worn acacia-print rug, her shoulders still damp from snow. She paused before one of Noelhard's Wiiralt forgeries on the wall—the shooter's gaze pierced the darkness, drilling into the blackened eyes of the Berber man whose mouth was twisted into a sly grin. Focused and determined, she returned to the front room and shot each criminal in the back of the head once more to be on the safe side. Butterball was still alive, gasping and pleading, but Murka showed no mercy. Again, she paused to stare at the shelves laden with thousands of books that contained uncounted lives and incredible twists of fate. The higher her gaze drifted and ascended through the bizarre, unfashionable cathedral, the more she grasped that even a Chekist can possess emotions and erudition. She longed for springs and summers that could spirit her away from this dreadful Baltic province, remove her from the whole odious and inexplicably earthly task code-named "Gogol." She picked up her pace. A small old-fashioned oil lamp that Noelhard kept burning all night in the store window to prevent passersby from discerning much inside briefly illuminated the snowy street and the Chekist's sky-colored vehicle. The lamp suddenly aged centuries, cracked, toppled to the floor as if shoved, and exploded in a ball of flame like a rapidly fading memory.

Viljandi's blazing antique bookstore resembled a giant page-lined stove. The books combusted, but Murka's engine wouldn't start. Without warning, the world started shaking as if trucks were rolling past. The incredible vibration, like a seabed being scraped by hundreds of backhoes, made the full length of Castle Street shimmer anew. An ocher-toned supernatural force penetrated one end of the thoroughfare: the colossal yellow metal cigar with bloody periscopes protruding from its surface flattened streetlights and gashed façades as it floated by. Red lights beamed from the periscopes, raking the surroundings as they searched like freakish drainpipes come to life. Spinning like vinyl records, the submarine's two propellers broke windows and smashed heavy stone balconies to smithereens. The majestic brick corner tower that had graced postcards of Viljandi in every era of social rule crumbled, bits of rooftile soaring through the air like flying fish. Horrified, Murka stared in the rearview mirror as the bewildering, accursed yellow wall drew closer and closer, crushing everything before it like a diver plummeting into a well. The destructive spectacle crept unstoppably towards the bookstore. With a screech, the car roof started to cave in. Murka desperately attempted to open the door so as not to be caught between dashboard and seat like a goldfish in a mud puddle, but the inhuman pressure bearing down on the vehicle suddenly ceased. The yellow cigar came to a stop directly above her. A narrow gangway with flowers as rivets was lowered from on high. Then, the door of the burning bookstore slowly swung open, though no one emerged.

The Duel at the Restaurant

Amid the general mayhem of museum pieces being hauled into the restaurant by order of the almighty Vanska, no one noticed the almost imperceptible fluctuation in the weights of the mundane and the divine. A luxury wardrobe was placed squarely in the center of the dancefloor and, in the protracted din, no one heard the furious knocking coming from within or a muffled voice demanding justice. The key finally shot out of the keyhole with a force that would have made a body-builder double over or have blinded anyone peering in through the window. The second the door swung open, Mr. Squall fired hitting Arkasha dead in the heart on stage, like an almond tree in blossom striking a lone wayfarer as he crosses a perilous mountain path filled with all types of horrors. For a moment, the two men of childlike stature stared at each other in bewilderment before one fell dead to the ground. Arkasha's singing had ceased for all eternity. Just as the impermanent becomes permanent and the mortal immortal, the astonished Mr. Squall stood sinisterly grasping a smoking rifle in the blinding lights. He had a fleeting sense of home—all his copper dishes and the trinkets for which he'd longed so dearly were glittering around him. The memory would have held fast in his mind forever, had the glass-eyed waiter-bouncer not flung Mr. Squall headfirst into a large mirror and oblivion.

At the Foot of the Cross

What's written in the Gospels—that in the end, only women remained at the foot of the Prophet's cross—acquired eternal and unalterable significance that night in Viljandi. When Zinaida and Natasha arrived at the plundered museum, they saw the heavy iron door had been lifted off its hinges. The museum was empty!

Zinaida ran into the spacious living room where she had spent so many blissful hours at the card table, and fell to the ground in tears. Natasha stood in the hallway, also sobbing. Was there no longer justice and order in the world? How could it be possible for a state museum to be . . . and by the orders of some man named Vanska . . .

Katerina was helping Gogol up the stairs. Natasha saw them coming and turned away.

"Woman, why are you crying? Whom do you seek?" Gogol asked, unsteady on his feet, gripping the banister tightly. Natasha couldn't bring herself to answer. Katerina and Katya helped her and the old man inside.

Gogol seemed to feel at ease in the dim room without

electric lighting, and headed straight into the dark toilet. All the women were crying; Zinaida had begun
picking up scraps of wallpaper. It all seemed utterly
pointless and unjust. But then, Gogol reemerged, stood
among them, and spoke: "Just as I was awoken and sent
here to you, so will I dispatch you as well!" He blew
upon them and the women felt miraculous relief, in
spite of the dreadful stench.

Zinaida went into the kitchen and discovered the
teapot was still there. Katya and Katerina comforted
Natasha, who couldn't believe the great Gogol himself
was standing before her. She'd heard on a television program that Gogol had been buried headless, like John
the Baptist, but this man still had his head on his shoulders and, furthermore, he was somewhat unpleasantly
shriveled and foul-smelling. Katerina spoke convincingly
and the woman soon came to believe her. Also, the living Gogol would be an unbelievable attraction, muse-
um-wise! She could already imagine a program for older
classes, in which the great classic would rise from a coffin and tell the children about his life. The guide should
be somewhat reserved and agreeably timid—now *that*
would be quite the show of literary history! Or what
about an ideologically-correct tour of Viljandi with
Gogol? Not even Moscow's famous Bulgakov Museum
with its red double-decker bus could come anywhere
close! Natasha's mood started to improve, and she began
making mental notes. Every word that escaped Gogol's
lips seemed worth its weight in gold; worthy of searing
into a wooden tablet. When dawn began to creep over

the horizon, she called Petrusha and asked the boy's help in decorating the room. In a bizarre turn, she suddenly felt profoundly and feverishly fond of him! Zinaida simply sighed. Luckily, there was still a pack of cards in her work gown and, for the first time in many a long year, she felt that now, immediately, this very day, she could retire.

Light cascaded through the windows and Gogol lay down on the wooden floor. He weakly beckoned Katerina.

"Do you love me more than these others?" he asked. Katerina said nothing, but nodded in spite of herself.

"Then take word to Opiatovich—my time is coming to an end. Follow me!" A strange substance that was neither blood nor saliva trickled from the corner of Gogol's mouth. Leaning over him, Natasha realized that if she were to record everything that had happened there that day, the volumes would be too many for the world.

Murka arrived at daybreak. Neither the women nor Petrusha had been capable of hanging the heavy iron door back on its hinges, so anyone could still walk in. The young artist had spent several hours painting a dramatic coffin on the floor around Gogol. Murka touched Gogol's hand, but her pass-grip slipped. She stabbed a knife into his side; blood and water spilled out. Gogol was as dead as could be, in any case. Murka lifted the sheet—his shinbones were very frail. She snapped them softly.

The chittering of lovebirds was coming from behind the kitchen door—Natasha and Petrusha were

PAAVO MATSIN

PAAVO MATSIN

GOGOL'S DISCO

PAAVO MATSIN

"*All-yew-need-iz-laav!*" he declared in warm saluta-
tion before popping a pellet of bread in his mouth.
By then, everyone had noticed his muddy aircraft that
hung suspended above the well outside, bristling like a
giant unearthly bladder with clumps of mud plastered
to its sides.

At the same time, the four new evangelists were
sitting in the spacious common room of the Jämejala
Asylum: Noelhard Spring, Konstantin Opiatovich,
Grigori Cuffovich, and, slightly withdrawn from the
rest, the dispirited Katerina. She would have greatly
preferred to be back working at the Novel.

No less unpleasant to her was the fact that the men's
and women's toilets there were no longer segregated.

"Now *that's* a real breakthrough, huh?! Androgyny!"
Noelhard had crowed in praise of the news.

Special rules were indeed in place in the evangelists'
wing, which was frequented by a number of important
guests. Even at that very moment, Noelhard was helping the conductor Vanska climb out of a shungite bath.
According to new regulations at the madhouse, all the
blue-department agents who had interrogated Noelhard
were required to carry a strange black "apsis stone" in
their leather haversacks for disinfecting water, everywhere and always. The new directive was issued after
a general had spoken with Noelhard and ultimately
agreed to try his shungite sofa, which convinced him
that that little stone could still be the glorious Empire's
salvation.

"You wouldn't by any chance be inclined to amend

your gospel, would you?" Vanska asked as he lounged in the warm water.

"What for?"

"Well, I, for one, definitely don't agree with all the words you put in my mouth! When Arkasha took that bullet, I most certainly did not remark that he'd been given 'a third eye and an Indian ventilation shaft between the other two'—I said nothing of the sort! He was shot in the heart, I tell you!"

Noelhard smirked. Vanska's legs glowed in the dark shungite water like two stout and very precious drainpipes.

"Alas, it's too late," Vanska sighed, reluctant to argue at any greater length. "Not even the commoners in Moscow talk of anything else anymore—all you hear is Gogol of Viljandi and his teachings!"

"What about shungite?!" cried Noelhard. "Hasn't its fame spread with the gospel? I did cover the topic extensively . . . Do Muscovites bathe with it? Do they use the miracle stone to purify water?"

The great conductor climbed out of the bathtub. Bliss suddenly descended upon him.

"Yes, Noelhard. The Tsar himself bathes in it!"

Vanska rubbed his reddened eyes and added in a silky, fluid bass:

"And he even reads that new Gogol-shungite gospel of yours like a babe spooning up kasha."

Glossary

aranzhirovchik: fixer (Russian)

baranka: a small hard-baked bread ring common throughout Eastern Europe

biznezmen: businessmen (Russian)

blatnoi (masc. adj.), *blatnaya* (fem. adj.), *blatnyak* (n.): pertaining to, member of an often romanticized Russian criminal subculture

bouquiniste: secondhand bookseller (French)

brodyak: tramp, vagabond (Russian)

bumashnik: wallet (Russian)

chanson: in Russian culture, a musical genre commonly involving singer-songwriters and criminal themes

Chekist: member of the Cheka (ChK), the Bolshevik secret police, an organization that investigated counter-revolutionaries and executed real and alleged enemies of Lenin's regime from 1917 to 1922, forerunner of the OGPU and NKVD

depresyak: bout of depression (Russian)

divanchik: sofa (diminutive) (Russian)

dukh: soul (Russian)

durak: fool, idiot (Russian)

Estonian Forest Brothers: a partisan group that waged guerilla war against the Soviet regime in the early years of Soviet occupation

Estonka: Estonian female (Russian)

finka: Finnish knife (Russian)

gorodok: small town (Russian)

Hauff, Wilhelm (1802–1827): German poet and novelist

Hekhalot: genre of Jewish esoteric and revelatory texts

hopak: Ukrainian folk dance

kamorka: tiny room, closet (Russian)

karmanchik: pickpocket (Russian)

kasha: buckwheat porridge (Russian)

khorosho: good, fine (Russian)

Khottabych: a genie in a Russian children's story by Lazar Lagin (1903–1979)

Khrushchyovka: a low-cost brick or concrete-panel apartment building, the style of which developed during the Soviet era under Nikita Khrushchev

knyaz: prince (Russian)

konyets: (the) end (Russian)

koroche: so, anyway, to cut a long story short (Russian)

korona: crown (Russian)

kostyumchik: suit-wearer (Russian)

Kronstadt: a Russian city and maritime defense center in the Gulf of Finland; the Kronstadt sea-gauge is used in Russia to measure all depths and altitudes

kut'ya: sweet grain dish served during the Christmas holidays and at funerals (Russian)

kvakushka: wah-wah pedal (or the sound made by one) (Russian)

Lake Pskovskoye: Russian name for the lower portion of Lake Peipus (Estonian Peipsi), after the large town of Pskov (Estonian Pihkva)

lyubov': love (Russian)

mamochka: mommy (Russian)

militsiya: Russian police forces

Misha the Bear: the Russian mascot of the 1980 Moscow Olympic Games

"Murka": song popular among Russian criminals

muzykant: musician (Russian)

nauka: science, knowledge (Russian)

nemodny: unstylish (Russian)

Oy, blyad'!: Oh, fuck (literally: "whore")! (Russian)

Palace Square: *(Russian Dvortsovaya ploshchad)* the central city square of St. Petersburg, Russia

pampushky: small Ukrainian raised buns

parasha: prison-cell toilet, shitter, by extension, the lowest of the low (Russian) *pelmen*: savory Russian dumpling

Poruchik Rhzevsky: a category of crude Russian jokes involving a cavalry officer

"*Privet, rebyata!*": Hi, guys! (Russian)

prostoye: simple (Russian)

pryanik: sweet baked Eastern European treats

Pugacheva, Alla (1959-): Russian singer

Rostova, Natasha: character in Tolstoy's *War and Peace*

ryba: fish (Russian)

Severny, Arkady Dmitrievich (1939–1980): a popular Russian chanson singer-songwriter

sbornik: collection, anthology (Russian)

shayka: gang (Russian)

Shekhinah: the Jewish dwelling or setting of the divine presence of God

sident: inmate (Russian)

skazka: fairytale (Russian)

stilyaga: (Soviet-era) dandy, fashionista, beatnik (Russian)

studyent: student (Russian)

Tsarskoye Selo: former Russian Imperial residence to the south of St. Petersburg

unitaz: flush toilet (Russian)

ushanka: Russian cap with earflaps

vareniki: filled Ukrainian dumplings

vechnoe: everlasting (Russian)

Viljandi: town in central-southwest Estonia

volyushka: freedom (diminutive) (Russian)

von Glehn, Nikolai (1841–1923): a Baltic German landowner and manor lord who founded the Estonian town of Nõmme (now a suburb of Tallinn)

Vysotsky, Vladimir (1938–1980): legendary Russian actor, poet, and singer-songwriter

Wiiralt, Eduard (1898–1954): a renowned Estonian graphic artist

yeli-yeli: barely (Russian)

yerundisha: fiasco (Russian)

zamok: key (Russian)

zapaska: hem (Russian)

Murka

Pribylá v Odéssu bánda iz Amúra,
Býli v bánde úrki, shulerá.
Bánda zanimálas' tyómnymi dyelámi
I za nyéy sledílo Gub Che Ká!
Verkh derzhála bába – zváli yeyó Múrka,
khítraya i smélaya bylá.
Dázhe zlýye úrki i tyé boyális' Múrku,
Vorovskúyu zhizn' oná velá.

Vot poshlí prostály, nachalís' obvály.
Mnógo stálo v bánde popadát'.

Kak naytí skoréye, któ zhe stál shalyávym,
Chtóby za izménu pokarát'.
Raz poshlí na délo, výpit' zakhotélos',
I zashlí v shikárnyy restorán.
Tam sidéla Múrka, v kózhanoy tuzhúrke,
A iz-pod pólu torchál nagán.

Zdrávstvuy, moyá Múrka! Zdrávstvuy, dorogáya!
Rázve zh yá tebyá nye odyevál!
Kól'tsa i brasléty, yúbki i zhakéty,
Rázve zh yá tebyé ne pokupál.
Zdrávstvuy, moy Múrka! Zdrávstvuy, dorogáya!
Zdrávstvuy, moy Múrka i proshcháy!
Ty zashukherila vsyu náshu malínu,
A tepér' maslínu poluch">áy!